Acclaim for

ali smith

the first person and
other stories

"Always imaginative, deftly written, and often funny to a fault, *The First Person and Other Stories* is a dizzying collection of stories by a writer unafraid. Sometimes inexplicable, always mesmerizing, Smith's collection embraces the disorder of living as it embraces the joys of being a writer."
—*The Anniston Star*

"*The First Person and Other Stories* targets the romantic poseurs in all of us."　　　　—*Vogue*

"Everyone has their own tale to tell in this bang-up collection. . . . At once quirky and compulsively readable, this collection puts a layered and enjoyable spin on the many forms of the short story."
—*Publishers Weekly*

ali smith

the first person and
other stories

Ali Smith is the author of six previous
works of fiction, including the novel *Hotel
World*, which was shortlisted for both the
Orange Prize and the Man Booker Prize
and won the Encore Award and the Scottish
Arts Council Book of the Year Award, and
The Accidental, which won the Whitbread
Award and was shortlisted for the Man
Booker Prize and the Orange Broadband
Prize for Fiction. Her story collections
include *Free Love*, which won a Saltire
Society First Book of the Year Award and
a Scottish Arts Council Award, and *The
Whole Story and Other Stories*. Born in
Inverness, Scotland, in 1962, Smith now
lives in Cambridge, England.

ali smith

the first person and
other stories

ali smith

the first person and other stories

ANCHOR BOOKS

A DIVISION OF RANDOM HOUSE, INC.

NEW YORK

FIRST ANCHOR BOOKS EDITION, JANUARY 2010

Grateful acknowledgment is made to Farrar, Straus and Giroux, LLC for permission to reprint an excerpt from "The First Person" from *Being Again: Collected Poems by Grace Paley*, copyright © 2000 by Grace Paley. Reprinted by permission of Farrar, Straus and Giroux, LLC.

The Library of Congress has cataloged the Pantheon edition as follows:
Smith, Ali.
The first person and other stories / Ali Smith.
p. cm.
I. Title.
PR6069.M4213F57 2009
823'.914—dc22   2008036024

Anchor ISBN: 978-0-307-45485-0

www.anchorbooks.com

10 9 8 7 6 5 4 3 2 1
147429898

acknowledgements and thanks

Thank you to the following publications where stories from this collection first appeared:

Prospect, The Brighton Book
The Times, Tales of the Decongested
Carlos, The Scotsman
Secrets, The Guardian

'Writ' was first commissioned and published in a limited numbered edition of 200 by The Oundle Press

'True short story' was originally written in 2005 in playful response to a speech given by *Prospect*'s deputy editor Alex Linklater on the inauguration of the National Short Story Prize. It was published

by *Prospect* in December 2005 and has been
slightly updated for inclusion in this collection

Thank you, Simon
Thank you, Andrew, and thank you, Tracy
and everybody at Wylie's
Thank you, Becky, and thank you, Xandra

Thank you, Kasia
Thank you, Mary
Thank you, Sarah

for Sarah Wood
(I should be so lucky)

for Kasia Boddy
(on the sunny side of the street)

for Nicky Haire
(s'wonderful)

The first person is often the lover who
says I never knew anyone like you
The listener is the beloved She whispers
Who? Me?
Grace Paley

So many pieces of me! I must hold tight.
Edwin Morgan

True to oneself! Which self?
Katherine Mansfield

Our responsibility begins
with the power to imagine.
Haruki Murakami

contents

true short story

There were two men in the café at the table next to mine. One was younger, one was older. They could have been father and son, but there was none of that practised diffidence, none of the cloudy anger that there almost always is between fathers and sons. Maybe they were the result of a parental divorce, the father keen to be a father now that his son was properly into his adulthood, the son keen to be a man in front of his father now that his father was opposite him for at least the length of time of a cup of coffee. No. More likely the older man was the kind of family friend who provides a fathership on summer weekends for the small boy of a divorce-family; a man who knows his responsibility, and now look, the boy had grown up, the man was an older man, and there was this unsaid understanding between them, etc.

I stopped making them up. It felt a bit wrong to. Instead, I listened to what they were saying. They were talking about literature, which happens to be interesting to me, though it wouldn't interest a lot of people. The younger man was talking about the difference between the novel and the short story. The novel, he was saying, was a flabby old whore.

A flabby old whore! the older man said looking delighted.

She was serviceable, roomy, warm and familiar, the younger was saying, but really a bit used up, really a bit too slack and loose.

Slack and loose! the older said laughing.

Whereas the short story, by comparison, was a nimble goddess, a slim nymph. Because so few people had mastered the short story she was still in very good shape.

Very good shape! The older man was smiling from ear to ear at this. He was presumably old enough to remember years in his life, and not so long ago, when it would have been at least a bit dodgy to talk like this. I idly wondered how many of the books in my house were fuckable and how good they'd be in bed. Then I sighed, and got my mobile out and phoned my friend, with whom I usually go to this café on Friday mornings.

She knows quite a lot about the short story. She's spent a lot of her life reading them, writing about them, teaching them, even on occasion writing them. She's read more short stories than most people know (or care) exist. I suppose you could call it a lifelong act of love, though she's not very old, was that morning still in her late thirties. A life-so-far act of love. But already she knew more about the short story and about the people all over the world who write and have written short stories than anyone I've ever met.

She was in hospital, on this particular Friday a couple of years ago now, because a course of chemotherapy had destroyed every single one of her tiny white blood cells and after it had she'd picked up an infection in a wisdom tooth.

I waited for the automaton voice of the hospital phone system to tell me all about itself, then to recite robotically back to me the number I'd just called, then to mispronounce my friend's name, which is Kasia, then to tell me exactly how much it was charging me to listen to it tell me all this, and then to tell me how much it would cost to speak to my friend per minute. Then it connected me.

Hi, I said. It's me.

Are you on your mobile? she said. Don't, Ali, it's expensive on this system. I'll call you back.

No worries, I said. It's just a quickie. Listen. Is the short story a goddess and a nymph and is the novel an old whore?

Is what what? she said.

An old whore, kind of Dickensian one, maybe, I said. Like that prostitute who first teaches David Niven how to have sex in that book.

David Niven? she said.

You know, I said. The prostitute he goes to in The Moon's a Balloon when he's about fourteen, and she's really sweet and she initiates him and he loses his virginity, and he's still wearing his socks, or maybe that's the prostitute who's still wearing the socks, I can't remember, anyway, she's really sweet to him and then he goes back to see her in later life when she's an old whore and he's an internationally famous movie star, and he brings her a lot of presents because he's such a nice man and never forgets a kindness. And is the short story more like Princess Diana?

The short story like Princess Diana, she said. Right.

I sensed the two men, who were getting ready to leave the café, looking at me curiously. I held up my phone.

I'm just asking my friend what she thinks about your nymph thesis, I said.

Both men looked slightly startled. Then both men left the café without looking back.

I told her about the conversation I'd just overheard.

I was thinking of Diana because she's a bit nymphy, I suppose, I said. I can't think of a goddess who's like a nymph. All the goddesses that come into my head are, like, Kali, or Sheela-Na-Gig. Or Aphrodite, she was pretty tough. All that deer-slaying. Didn't she slay deer?

Why is the short story like a nymph, Kasia said. Sounds like a dirty joke. Ha.

Okay, I said. Come on then. Why is the short story like a nymph?

I'll think about it, she said. It'll give me something to do in here.

Kasia and I have been friends now for just over twenty years, which doesn't feel at all long, though it sounds quite long. 'Long' and 'short' are relative. What was long was every single day she was spending in hospital; today was her tenth long day in one of the cancer wards, being injected with a cocktail of antibiotics and waiting for her temperature to come down and her white cell count to go up. When those two tiny personal adjustments happened in the world, then she'd be allowed to go home. Also, there was a lot of sadness round her in the ward. After ten long days the heaviness of that sadness, which might sound bearably small if you're not a person who has to think about it or is being forced by circumstance to address it, but is close to epic if you are, was considerable.

She phoned me back later that afternoon and left a message on the answerphone. I could hear the clanking hospital and the voices of other people in the ward in the recorded air around her voice.

Okay. Listen to this. It depends what you mean by 'nymph'. So, depending. A short story is like a nymph because satyrs want to sleep with it all the time. A short story is like a nymph because both like to live on mountains and in groves and by springs and rivers and in valleys and cool grottoes. A short story is like a nymph because it likes to accompany Artemis on her travels. Not very funny yet, I know, but I'm working on it.

I heard the phone being hung up. Message received at three forty-three, my answerphone's robot voice said. I called her back and went through the exact echo of the morning's call to the system. She answered and before I could even say hello she said:

Listen! Listen! A short story is like a nymphomaniac because both like to sleep around

– or get into lots of anthologies – but neither accepts money for the pleasure.

I laughed out loud.

Unlike the bawdy old whore, the novel, ha ha, she said. And when I was speaking to my father at lunchtime he told me you can fish for trout with a nymph. They're a kind of fishing fly. He says there are people who carry magnifying glasses around with them all the time in case they get the chance to look at real nymphs, so as to be able to copy them even more exactly in the fishing flies they make.

I tell you, I said. The world is full of astounding things.

I know, she said. What do you reckon to the anthology joke?

Six out of ten, I said.

Rubbish then, she said. Okay. I'll try and think of something better.

Maybe there's mileage in the nymphs-at-your-flies thing, I said.

Ha ha, she said. But I'll have to leave the nymph thing this afternoon and get back on the Herceptin trail.

God, I said.

I'm exhausted, she said. We're drafting letters.

When is an anti-cancer drug not an anti-cancer drug? I said.

When people can't afford it, she said. Ha ha.

Lots of love, I said.

You too, she said. Cup of tea?

I'll make us one, I said. Speak soon.

I heard the phone go dead. I put my phone down and went through and switched the kettle on. I watched it reach the boil and the steam come out of the spout. I filled two cups with boiling water and dropped the teabags in. I drank my tea watching the steam rise off the other cup.

This is what Kasia meant by 'Herceptin trail'.

Herceptin is a drug that's been being used in breast cancer treatment for a while now. Doctors had, at the point in time that Kasia and I were having the conversations in this story, very recently discovered that it really helps some women – those who over-produce the HER2 protein – in the early stages of the disease. When given to a receptive case it can cut the risk of the cancer returning by 50 per cent. Doctors all over the world were excited about it because it amounted to a paradigm shift in breast cancer treatment.

I had never heard of any of this till Kasia told me, and she had never heard of any of it until a small truth, less than two centimetres in size, which a doctor found in April that year in one of her breasts, had meant a paradigm shift in everyday life. It was now August. In May her doctor had told her about how good Herceptin is, and how she'd definitely be able to have it at the end of her chemotherapy on the NHS. Then at the end of July her doctor was visited by a member of the PCT, which stands for the words Primary, Care and Trust, and is concerned with NHS funding. The PCT member instructed my friend's doctor not to tell any more of the women affected in the hospital's catchment area about the wonders of Herceptin until a group called NICE had approved its cost-effectiveness. At the time, they thought this might take about nine months or maybe a year (by which time it would be too late for my friend and many other women). Though Kasia knew that if she wanted to buy Herceptin on BUPA, right then, for roughly twenty-seven thousand pounds, she could. This kind of thing will be happening to an urgently needed drug right now, somewhere near you.

'Primary'. 'Care'. 'Trust'. 'Nice'.

Here's a short story that most people already think they know about a nymph. (It also happens to be one of the earliest manifestations in literature of what we now call anorexia.)

Echo was an Oread, which is a kind of mountain nymph. She was well known among the nymphs and shepherds not just for her glorious garrulousness but for her ability to save her nymph friends from the wrath of the goddess Juno. For instance, her friends would be lying about on the hillside in the sun and Juno would come round the corner, about to catch them slacking, and Echo, who had a talent for knowing when Juno was about to turn up, would leap to her feet and head the goddess off by running up to her and distracting her with stories and talk, talk and stories, until all the slacker nymphs were up and working like they'd never been slacking at all.

When Juno worked out what Echo was doing she was a bit annoyed. She pointed at her with her curse-finger and threw off the first suitable curse that came into her head.

From now on, she said, you will be able only to repeat out loud the words you've heard others say just a moment before. Won't you?

Won't you, Echo said.

Her eyes grew large. Her mouth fell open.

That's you sorted, Juno said.

You sordid, Echo said.

Right. I'm off back to the hunt, Juno said.

The cunt, Echo said.

Actually, I'm making up that small rebellion. There is actually no rebelliousness for Echo in Ovid's original version of the story. It seems that after she's robbed of being able to talk on her own terms, and of being able to watch her friends' backs for them, there's nothing left for her – in terms of story – but to fall in love with a boy so in love with himself that he spends all his days bent over a pool of his own desire and eventually pines to near-death (then transforms, instead of dying, from a boy into a little white flower).

Echo pined too. Her weight dropped off her. She became fashionably skinny, then she became nothing but bones, then all that was left of her was a whiny, piny voice which floated bodilessly about, saying over and over exactly the same things that everybody else was saying.

Here, by contrast, is the story of the moment I met my friend Kasia, more than twenty years ago.

I was a postgraduate student at Cambridge and I had lost my voice. I don't mean I'd lost it because I had a cold or a throat infection, I mean that two years of a system of hierarchies so entrenched that girls and women were still a bit of a novelty to it had somehow knocked what voice I had out of me.

So I was sitting at the back of a room not even really listening properly any more, and I heard a voice. It was from somewhere up ahead of me. It was a girl's voice and it was directly asking the person giving the seminar and the chair of the seminar a question about the American writer Carson McCullers.

Because it seems to me that McCullers is obviously very relevant at all levels in this discussion, the voice said.

The person and the chair of the meeting both looked a bit shocked that anyone had said anything out loud. The chair cleared his throat.

I found myself leaning forward. I hadn't heard anyone speak like this, with such an open and carefree display of knowledge and forthrightness, for a couple of years. More: earlier that day I had been talking with an undergraduate student who had been unable to find anyone in the whole of Cambridge University English Department to supervise her dissertation on McCullers. It seemed nobody eligible to teach had read her.

Anyway, I venture to say you'll find McCullers not at all of the same stature, the person giving the paper on Literature After Henry James said.

Well, the thing is, I disagree, the voice said.

I laughed out loud. It was a noise never heard in such a room; heads turned to see who was making such an unlikely noise. The new girl carried on politely asking questions which no one answered. She mentioned, I remember, how McCullers had been fond of a maxim: nothing human is alien to me.

At the end of the seminar I ran after that girl. I stopped her in the street. It was winter. She was wearing a red coat.

She told me her name. I heard myself tell her mine.

Franz Kafka says that the short story is a cage in search of a bird. (Kafka's been dead for more than eighty years, but I can still say Kafka says. That's just one of the ways art deals with our mortality.)

Tzvetan Todorov says that the thing about a short story is that it's so short it doesn't allow us the time to forget that it's only literature and not actually life.

Nadine Gordimer says short stories are absolutely about the present moment, like the brief flash of a number of fireflies here and there in the dark.

Elizabeth Bowen says the short story has the advantage over the novel of a special kind of concentration, and that it creates narrative every time absolutely on its own terms.

Eudora Welty says that short stories often problematize their own best interests and that this is what makes them interesting.

Henry James says that the short story, being so condensed, can give a particularized perspective on both complexity and continuity.

Jorge Luis Borges says that short stories can be the perfect form for novelists too lazy to write anything longer than fifteen pages.

Ernest Hemingway says that short stories are made by their own change and movement, and that even when a story seems static and you can't make out any movement in it at all it is probably changing and moving regardless, just unseen by you.

William Carlos Williams says that the short story, which acts like the flare of a match struck in the dark, is the only real form for describing the briefness, the brokenness and the simultaneous wholeness of people's lives.

Walter Benjamin says that short stories are stronger than the real, lived moment, because they can go on releasing the real, lived moment after the real, lived moment is dead.

Cynthia Ozick says that the difference between a short story and a novel is that the novel is a book whose journey, if it's a good working novel, actually alters a reader, whereas a short story is more like the talismanic gift given to the protagonist of a fairy tale – something complete, powerful, whose power may not yet be understood, which can be held in the hands or tucked into the pocket and taken through the forest on the dark journey.

Grace Paley says that she chose to write only short stories in her life because art is too long and life is too short, and that short stories are, by nature, about life, and that life itself is always found in dialogue and argument.

Alice Munro says that every short story is at least two short stories.

There were two men in the café at the table next to mine. One was younger, one was older. We sat in the same café for only a brief amount of time but we disagreed long enough for me to know there was a story in it.

This story was written in discussion with my friend Kasia, and in celebration of her (and all) tireless articulacy – one of the reasons, in this instance, that a lot more people were able to have that particular drug when they needed it.

So when is the short story like a nymph?

When the echo of it answers back.

the child

I went to Waitrose as usual in my lunchbreak to get the weekly stuff. I left my trolley by the vegetables and went to find bouquet garni for the soup. But when I came back to the vegetables again I couldn't find my trolley. It seemed to have been moved. In its place was someone else's shopping trolley, with a child sitting in the little child seat, its fat little legs through the leg-places.

Then I glanced into the trolley in which the child was sitting and saw in there the few things I'd already picked up: the three bags of oranges, the apricots, the organic apples, the folded copy of the Guardian and the tub of Kalamata olives. They were definitely my things. It was definitely my trolley.

The child in it was blond and curly-haired, very

fair-skinned and flushed, big-cheeked like a cupid or a chub-fingered angel on a Christmas card or a child out of an old-fashioned English children's book, the kind of book where they wear sunhats to stop themselves getting sunstroke all the post-war summer. This child was wearing a little blue tracksuit with a hood and blue shoes and was quite clean, though a little crusty round the nose. Its lips were very pink and perfectly bow-shaped; its eyes were blue and clear and blank. It was an almost embarrassingly beautiful child.

Hello, I said. Where's your mother?

The child looked at me blankly.

I stood next to the potatoes and waited for a while. There were people shopping all round. One of them had clearly placed this child in my trolley and when he or she came to push the trolley away I could explain these were my things and we could swap trolleys or whatever and laugh about it and I could get on with my shopping as usual.

I stood for five minutes or so. After five minutes I wheeled the child in the trolley to the Customer Services desk.

I think someone somewhere may be looking for this, I said to the woman behind the desk, who was busy on a computer.

Looking for what, Madam? she said.

I presume you've had someone losing their mind over losing him, I said. I think it's a him. Blue for a boy, etc.

The Customer Services woman was called Marilyn Monroe. It said so on her name-badge.

Quite a name, I said pointing to the badge.

I'm sorry? she said.

Your name, I said. You know. Monroe. Marilyn.

Yes, she said. That's my name.

She looked at me like I was saying something dangerously foreign-sounding to her.

How exactly can I help you? she said in a sing-song voice.

Well, as I say, this child, I said.

What a lovely boy! she said. He's very like his mum.

Well, I wouldn't know, I said. He's not mine.

Oh, she said. She looked offended. But he's so like you. Aren't you? Aren't you, darling? Aren't you, sweetheart?

She waved the curly red wire attached to her keyring at the child, who watched it swing inches away from its face, nonplussed. I couldn't imagine what she meant. The child looked nothing like me at all.

No, I said. I went round the corner to get something and when I got back to my trolley he was there, in it.

Oh, she said. She looked very surprised. We've had no reports of a missing child, she said.

She pressed some buttons on an intercom thing.

Hello? she said. It's Marilyn on Customers. Good, thanks, how are you? Anything up there on a missing child? No? Nothing on a child? Missing, or lost? Lady here claims she found one.

She put the intercom down. No, Madam, I'm afraid nobody's reported any child that's lost or missing, she said.

A small crowd had gathered behind us. He's adorable, one woman said. Is he your first?

He's not mine, I said.

How old is he? another said.

I don't know, I said.

You don't? she said. She looked shocked.

Aw, he's lovely, an old man, who seemed rather too poor a person to be shopping in Waitrose, said. He got a fifty-pence piece out of his pocket, held it up to me and said: Here you are. A piece of silver for good luck.

He tucked it into the child's shoe.

I wouldn't do that, Marilyn Monroe said. He'll get it out of there and swallow it and choke on it.

He'll never get it out of there, the old man said. Will you? You're a lovely boy. He's a lovely boy, he is. What's your name? What's his name? I bet you're like your dad. Is he like his dad, is he?

I've no idea, I said.

No idea! the old man said. Such a lovely boy! What a thing for his mum to say!

No, I said. Really. He's nothing to do with me, he's not mine. I just found him in my trolley when I came back with the –

At this point the child sitting in the trolley looked at me, raised its little fat arms in the air and said, straight at me: Mammuum.

Everybody round me in the little circle of baby admirers looked at me. Some of them looked knowing and sly. One or two nodded at each other.

The child did it again. It reached its arms up, almost as if to pull itself up out of the trolley seat and lunge straight at me through the air.

Mummaam, it said.

The woman called Marilyn Monroe picked up her intercom again and spoke into it. Meanwhile the child had started to cry. It screamed and bawled. It shouted its word for mother at me over and over again and shook the trolley with its shouting.

Give him your car keys, a lady said. They love to play with car keys.

Bewildered, I gave the child my keys. It threw

them to the ground and screamed all the more.

Lift him out, a woman in a Chanel suit said. He just wants a little cuddle.

It's not my child, I explained again. I've never seen it before in my life.

Here, she said.

She pulled the child out of the wire basket of the trolley seat, holding it at arm's length so her little suit wouldn't get smeared. It screamed even more as its legs came out of the wire seat; its face got redder and redder and the whole shop resounded with the screaming. (I was embarrassed. I felt peculiarly responsible. I'm so sorry, I said to the people round me.) The Chanel woman shoved the child hard into my arms. Immediately it put its arms around me and quietened to fretful cooing.

Jesus Christ, I said because I had never felt so powerful in all my life.

The crowd round us made knowing noises. See? a woman said. I nodded. There, the old man said. That'll always do it. You don't need to be scared, love. Such a pretty child, a passing woman said. The first three years are a nightmare, another said, wheeling her trolley past me towards the fine wines. Yes, Marilyn Monroe was saying into the intercom. Claiming it wasn't. Hers. But I think it's all right now. Isn't it Madam? All right now? Madam?

Yes, I said through a mouthful of the child's blond hair.

Go on home, love, the old man said. Give him his supper and he'll be right as rain.

Teething, a woman ten years younger than me said. She shook her head; she was a veteran. It can drive you crazy, she said, but it's not forever. Don't worry. Go home now and have a nice cup of herb tea and it'll all settle down, he'll be asleep as soon as you know it.

Yes, I said. Thanks very much. What a day.

A couple of women gave me encouraging smiles; one patted me on the arm. The old man patted me on the back, squeezed the child's foot inside its shoe. Fifty pence, he said. That used to be ten shillings. Long before your time, little soldier. Used to buy a week's worth of food, ten shillings did. In the old days, eh? Ah well, some things change and some others never do. Eh? Eh, Mum?

Yes. Ha ha. Don't I know it, I said shaking my head.

I carried the child out into the car park. It weighed a ton.

I thought about leaving it right there in the car park behind the recycling bins, where it couldn't do too much damage to itself and someone would easily find it before it starved or anything. But I knew that if I did this the people in the store would remember me and track me down after all the fuss we'd just had. So I laid it on the back seat of the car, buckled it in with one of the seatbelts and the blanket off the back window, and got in the front. I started the engine.

I would drive it out of town to one of the villages, I decided, and leave it there, on a doorstep or outside a shop or something, when no one was looking, where someone else would report it found and its real parents or whoever had lost it would be able to claim it back. I would have to leave it somewhere without being seen, though, so no one would think I was abandoning it.

Or I could simply take it straight to the police. But then I would be further implicated. Maybe the police would think I had stolen the child, especially now that I had left the supermarket openly carrying it as if it were mine after all.

I looked at my watch. I was already late for work.

I cruised out past the garden centre and towards the motorway and decided I'd turn left at the first signpost and deposit it in the first quiet, safe, vaguely-peopled place I found then race back into town. I stayed in the inside lane and watched for village signs.

You're a really rubbish driver, a voice said from the back of the car. I could do better than that, and I can't even drive. Are you for instance representative of all women drivers or is it just you among all women who's so rubbish at driving?

It was the child speaking. But it spoke with so surprisingly charming a little voice that it made me want to laugh, a voice as young and clear as a series of ringing bells arranged into a pretty melody. It said the complicated words, representative and for instance, with an innocence that sounded ancient, centuries old, and at the same time as if it had only just discovered their meaning and was trying out their usage and I was privileged to be present when it did.

I slewed the car over to the side of the motorway, switched the engine off and leaned over the front seat into the back. The child still lay there helpless, rolled up in the tartan blanket, held in place by the seatbelt. It didn't look old enough to be able to speak. It looked barely a year old.

It's terrible. Asylum-seekers and foreigners come here and take all our jobs and all our benefits, it said preternaturally, sweetly. They should all be sent back to where they come from.

There was a slight endearing lisp on the *s* sounds in the words asylum and seekers and foreigners and jobs and benefits and sent.

What? I said.

Can't you hear? Cloth in your ears? it said. The real terrorists are people who aren't properly English. They will sneak into football stadiums and blow up innocent Christian people supporting innocent English teams.

The little words slipped out of its ruby-red mouth. I could just see the glint of its little coming teeth.

It said: The pound is our rightful heritage. We deserve our heritage. Women shouldn't work if they're going to have babies. Women shouldn't work at all. It's not the natural order of things. And as for gay weddings. Don't make me laugh.

Then it laughed, blondly, beautifully, as if only for me. Its big blue eyes were open and looking straight up at me as if I were the most delightful thing it had ever seen.

I was enchanted. I laughed back.

From nowhere a black cloud crossed the sun over its face, it screwed up its eyes and kicked its legs, waved its one free arm around outside the blanket, its hand clenched in a tiny fist, and began to bawl and wail.

It's hungry, I thought and my hand went down to my shirt and before I knew what I was doing I was unbuttoning it, getting myself out, and planning how to ensure the child's later enrolment in one of the area's better secondary schools.

I turned the car around and headed for home. I had decided to keep the beautiful child. I would feed it. I would love it. The neighbours would be amazed that I had hidden a pregnancy from them so well, and everyone would agree that the child was the most beautiful child ever to grace our street. My father would dandle the child on his knee. About time too, he'd say. I thought you were never going to make me a grandfather. Now I can die happy.

The beautiful child's melodious voice, in its pure RP pronunciation, the pronunciation of a child who's already been to an excellent public school and learned how exactly to speak, broke in on my dream.

Why do women wear white on their wedding day? it asked from the back of the car.

What do you mean? I said.

Why do women wear white on their wedding day? it said again.

Because white signifies purity, I said. Because it signifies –

To match the stove and the fridge when they get home, the child interrupted. An Englishman, an Irishman, a Chineseman and a Jew are all in an aeroplane flying over the Atlantic.

What? I said.

What's the difference between a pussy and a cunt? the child said in its innocent pealing voice.

Language! please! I said.

I bought my mother-in-law a chair, but she refused to plug it in, the child said. I wouldn't say my mother-in-law is fat, but we had to stop buying her Malcolm X t-shirts because helicopters kept trying to land on her.

I hadn't heard a fat mother-in-law joke for more than twenty years. I laughed. I couldn't not.

Why did they send premenstrual women into the desert to fight the Iraqis? Because they can retain water for four days. What do you call an Iraqi with a paper bag over his head?

Right, I said. That's it. That's as far as I go.

I braked the car and stopped dead on the inside lane. Cars squealed and roared past us with their drivers leaning on their horns. I switched on the hazard lights. The child sighed.

You're so politically correct, it said behind me charmingly. And you're a terrible driver. How do you make a woman blind? Put a windscreen in front of her.

Ha ha, I said. That's an old one.

I took the B roads and drove to the middle of a dense wood. I opened the back door of the car and bundled the beautiful blond child out. I locked the car. I carried the child for half a mile or so until I found a sheltered spot, where I left it in the tartan blanket under the trees.

I've been here before, you know, the child told me. S'not my first time.

Goodbye, I said. I hope wild animals find you and raise you well.

I drove home.

But all that night I couldn't stop thinking about the helpless child in the woods, in the cold, with nothing to eat and nobody knowing it was there. I got up at four a.m. and wandered round in my bedroom. Sick with worry, I drove back out to the wood road, stopped the car in exactly the same place and walked the half-mile back into the trees.

There was the child, still there, still wrapped in the tartan travel rug.

You took your time, it said. I'm fine, thanks for asking. I knew you'd be back. You can't resist me.

I put it in the back seat of the car again.

Here we go again. Where to now? the child said.

Guess, I said.

Can we go somewhere with broadband or wifi so I can look at some porn? the beautiful child said beautifully.

I drove to the next city and pulled into the first

supermarket car park I passed. It was 6.45 a.m. and it was open.

Ooh, the child said. My first 24-hour Tesco's. I've had an Asda and a Sainsbury's and a Waitrose but I've not been to a Tesco's before.

I pulled the brim of my hat down over my eyes to evade being identifiable on the CCTV and carried the tartan bundle in through the out doors when two other people were leaving. The supermarket was very quiet but there was a reasonable number of people shopping. I found a trolley, half-full of good things, French butter, Italian olive oil, a folded new copy of the Guardian, left standing in the biscuits aisle, and emptied the child into it out of the blanket, slipped its pretty little legs in through the gaps in the child-seat.

There you go, I said. Good luck. All the best. I hope you get what you need.

I know what you need all right, the child whispered after me, but quietly, in case anybody should hear. Psst, it hissed. What do you call a woman with two brain cells? Pregnant! Why were shopping trolleys invented? To teach women to walk on their hind legs!

Then it laughed its charming peal of a pure childish laugh and I slipped away out of the aisle and out of the doors past the shopgirls cutting open the plastic binding on the morning's new tabloids and arranging them on the newspaper shelves, and out of the supermarket, back to my car, and out of the car park, while all over England the bells rang out in the morning churches and the British birdsong welcomed the new day, God in his heaven, and all being right with the world.

present

There were only three people in The Inn: a man at the bar, the barmaid, and me. The man was chatting up the barmaid. The barmaid was polishing glasses. I was waiting for a pub supper I'd ordered half an hour ago. I was allowing myself one double whisky. It was a present to myself.

Have you seen them, covered in all the frost? the man was saying to the barmaid. Don't they look just like magic roofs, don't they look like winter always looked when you were a little child?

The barmaid ignored him. She held the glass up to the light to see if it was clean. She polished it some more. She held it up again.

The man gestured towards the pub's front window.

Go out and look at it. Just have a look at it, look at it on the roofs, the man said. Don't they look exactly like what winter was like when you were small? Like a white came over everything by magic, like a giant magician waved his hand and a white frost came down over everything.

You don't half talk a load of wank, the woman behind the bar said.

Her saying this made me laugh so suddenly that I choked on the drink I was taking. They both looked round. I coughed, turned away slightly towards the fire and went on looking at my paper like I was reading it.

I heard them shift their attention back towards each other.

It's Paula, isn't it? he said.

She said nothing.

It's definitely Paula, he said. I remember. I asked you before. Remember? I was here, I was in this very pub about six weeks ago. Remember?

She held another glass up and looked at it.

Well, I remember you, he said.

She put it down and picked up another. She held it up between her and the light.

So if you don't like Christmas and so on, Paula, he said. If you don't think it's a magic time from our childhoods and so on. Well, why'd you bother to decorate the pub, then? Why'd you bother to spray the snowy stuff on the door and the windows? Why'd you make the place look like snow off Christmas cards? It's only November. It's not even December.

It's not my pub, the woman said. I don't get to choose when Christmas begins and ends.

The whisky I'd choked on had gone down the wrong way and had formed a burning gutter along the inside of my windpipe. I ignored it. I read my paper. It was about how the Gulf Stream was being eroded at an almighty rate. Soon it would be as cold as Canada here in the winter. Soon the snow would be six feet high every winter and winters would last from October till April.

Magic roofs, the woman said. Christ. See the house with the Alfa Romeo outside it?

The man went to the door and opened it.

I can't see an Alfa Romeo from here, he said.

The third along car from the left, she said without raising her voice.

I saw some cars, but I'll take your word for it that one's an Alfa, he said coming back in.

They call him the German in the village, she said. His name's German-sounding. He never comes in here. He hit black ice round the Ranger Bend with his two sons in the car two years ago and the son that was in the front seat died. The car hasn't moved from outside that house since it came back from the garage with a new side on it. He walks to work, he walks out his gate and past it every day. We all go past it every day. It's filthy. It needs a good clean, just from sitting there in the weather. He had a German-sounding name and all, the son, I mean. He was eleven or twelve. He never came in here before it, the father I mean, the German, and he never comes in now. And the house next to his. That's where the girl lives who's in debt because of the pyramid.

Egypt? the man said.

Scheme, the woman said. Not to tell tales or nothing but I was at Asda and I heard her telling someone on her mobile that she had a dream.

The man leaned on the bar.

You're a dream, Paula, he said.

This is her dream, the woman said. Would you believe it. An angora jumper she'd bought on her credit card, listen to this, upped and left home because it was unhappy living with her. Then the jumper phoned her from the airport but because it couldn't speak, because jumpers can't, can they, she didn't know what it was trying to say.

An angry jumper? the man said.

No, an angora jumper, the woman said. It's a kind of wool, a warm expensive kind. And the house next to that. His daughter's a druggie. Whenever she comes back to the village he won't let her in the front door. First she throws stones at the living-room window. Then the old bloke calls the police. The house next to that. Divorced. He had an affair. She got custody. He's a nice guy. He works in the city. She's a teacher. She's got a Cinquecento.

She held up a glass, examined it against the light.

The house next to them, she said.

Uh huh? he said.

That's my house, she said.

You're not married, are you, Paula? the man said.

You are, the woman said. I can tell a mile off.

I'm not married, the man said. I'm as single as the day is long.

This time of year you'll be less single, then, she said.

You what? he said.

The days being shorter and all, the woman said.

What you laughing at? the man said. What you looking at?

He was talking to me. I pretended I hadn't heard or understood.

What's she think she's looking at? the man said.

Won't be long, the woman called over to me. Sorry to keep you waiting.

No worries, I said. It's fine.

She went through the door at the back. Have

you not thawed out the scampi? she was shouting as she went.

The man stared at me. There was quite a lot of hostility in his stare. I could feel it without me even looking back properly. When the woman came through from the kitchen and put down in front of me, like a firm promise that I would definitely be fed, condiments, and a knife and fork both neatly wrapped in a napkin, he shouted over at me from his place at the bar.

You agree with me. Don't you? *You* think it looks just like magic, he said. Like a magician off a TV programme when we were kids just, you know, waved his hand in the sky over all our home towns and down came the whiteness.

He started to come over; he looked like he might actually punch me if I said I disagreed. But when he reached the table I could see he was less drunk than he seemed. It was almost as if he was pretending to be more drunk than he was. He sat down on the stool across the table from me. He wasn't much older than me. His face was crumpled, like a piece of wrapping that someone has tried to squeeze in a fist into as small as possible a ball.

I looked down at my knife and fork wrapped in the napkin. There were little cartoon sprigs of holly all over the napkin.

The man picked the HP sauce bottle up out of the arrangement of salt and pepper and mustard and vinegar sachets and sauce bottles in front of me.

You know what the H and the P stand for on a bottle of HP? he said.

Houses of Parliament, I said.

His face fell. He looked truly disappointed that I knew. I pointed to the picture on the bottle's label. I shrugged.

You're not from round here, he said. Didn't think so, he said. Something about your shape of face. Don't get me wrong, he said. It's a nice shape of face. I'm from fifty miles from here, he said. Originally, I mean. What you drinking, then? he said.

He said it all very loudly, as if he was saying it not really to me but for the barmaid back behind the bar to hear.

How about I tell you, he said putting his foot up on the low stool nearest me, about what Christmas means to me? Shall I tell you two girls what a really happy Christmas is?

I looked at his foot in its scuffed shoe on the plush of the bar stool. I could see the colour of his socks. They were light brown. Someone had bought him these socks as a present, maybe, or maybe someone had bought them because he was lucky enough to have someone routinely care about his socks. Or, if not, he had gone into a shop and bought them himself. But this was the last thing I wanted to care about, a detail like where someone else's socks had come from. I had been out driving around since about half past four this morning. I had driven into the car park of this pub tonight precisely because I believed there would be nobody here I knew, nobody here who would bother me, nobody here who would ask anything of me, nobody here who would want to speak to me about anything, anything at all.

I looked at the man's foot again with the thin line of human skin there between the top of the sock and where the edge of his trouser leg began. I stood up. I got my car keys out of my pocket.

Going somewhere? the man said.

The barmaid was taking packets of peanuts off little hooks above the till, dusting them and putting them back. She turned as I went past.

Won't be much longer, five minutes at the most, she called after me.

I pushed the door open regardless and went out of The Inn.

But I was two new whiskys down, I realised as I slid into the driver's seat. I couldn't drive anywhere, not for a good while. I sat in the car in the lit car park and watched the sign that said The Inn hang motionless beyond the windscreen, which had immediately steamed up with the warmth coming off me. There was no wind tonight. That was why it was so frosty. It was cold out, bitterly cold. It would soon be bleak midwinter.

I put the key in the ignition and pushed the button which turns the seat-heating on. Cars were great. They were full of things that simply, mechanically, met people's needs. Inside seat-heating. Adjustable seat levers. Little vanity mirrors in the windscreen shades. Roof that slides right back if you want it to.

I began to try to guess what story the man would have told two virtual strangers in a pub to prove what made a good Christmas. The best Christmas lunch he'd ever eaten. The best present anyone ever gave him. It would be something about his childhood since that was all he'd really wanted to talk about in there, childhood and lost magic, and the coming back of magic at the coldest of times in the back of beyond in the form of a simple frost that catches the light in the dark.

Imagine if we had all been friends in that bar, had been people who really had something to say, had wanted to talk to each other.

Now you, I imagined the barmaid saying to me, perched on one of those too-high stools above me and him, so that leaning down and forking up one of my scampi pieces for herself is a little precarious, but she wavers perfectly, balances perfectly, tucks the scampi into her mouth and we all laugh together at her expertise, including herself.

Your turn, she says. A really happy one, come on.

Well, okay, though happy's not the word I'd have used at the time, I say. I'm about twelve.

I don't mean this to sound rude but you look a bit older than twelve, the man says.

Not now. Obviously. In the story, I say.

Okay, the man says.

Okay, the barmaid says.

And in my neighbourhood there's this new couple that's moved in a couple of streets down, and everybody knows them, everyone knows who they are, I mean, because they're a husband and wife teaching couple, they both teach modern languages at the school the local kids go to, the school I go to.

Not very Christmassy so far, the barmaid (Paula) says.

Give her a chance, the man says. She'll get to it. Some time in the near future.

Christmas past, Christmas present, Christmas near-future, Paula says.

Anyway, the Fenimores, Mr and Mrs Fenimore, I say. Mr Fenimore is really pioneering. He's small and slim, but always looks as if he's setting out on an adventure with an imaginary hiking stick in his hand.

I know the type, Paula says.

He takes over the after-school chess and judo clubs, I say. He starts up an after-school cookery class and he takes a lot of flak for being a man who runs a cookery class. Mrs Fenimore helps. She always helps. She is always there helping, she's a shy person who smiles a lot, while her husband, whom she looks at with eyes full of a sad, hopeful love, runs the school clubs, and not just those, he forms a neighbourhood wine club where our parents and the other neighbours who don't have kids go to the Fenimores' house to taste wine, Mrs Fenimore puts invitations through everybody's door, smiling shyly if you look out the window and see her on her rounds. JACK AND SHIRLEY FENIMORE INVITE YOU TO A SPECIAL WINE TASTING. Loads of people go, all the neighbours go, my mother and father go, and they never usually go to anything. They've never done anything like it before. Then everybody talks about how nice the Fenimores are, how much they like the Fenimores' house, car, garden, cutlery, design of plates. Then the Fenimores organize a theatre visit. JACK AND SHIRLEY FENIMORE INVITE YOU TO EDUCATING RITA AT THE EMPIRE. Everybody goes. JACK AND SHIRLEY FENIMORE INVITE YOU TO A MULLED WINE EXTRAVAGANZA. JACK AND SHIRLEY FENIMORE INVITE YOU ON A SOLSTICE ASSAULT ON BEN WYVIS.

Assault on Ben who? the man (I'll call him Tom) says.

No, I say. Ben Wyvis is a mountain. Ben is a Scottish word for mountain.

Yeah, I know, I know that, Tom says.

You don't know nothing, Paula says. You didn't know what angora was a minute ago.

Anyway, I say. About twenty of us, who've all lived under Ben Wyvis for most of our lives and have never been up it, seven or eight adults and the rest kids my age, some younger, a couple of older ones, get into a minibus the Fenimores hire, because Mr Fenimore's just got his minibus driving licence, and drive to the foot of Ben Wyvis to see how high up it we can get on the Sunday before Christmas, December 21st, a gloriously sunny Sunday, bright and crisp and blue-skied.

And then what happens?

Oh, okay, I get it, it's a game, Tom says. Okay. You get to the top and you have the most fantastic party and you kiss your first boy up a romantic mountain on the shortest day of the year.

The minibus breaks down, Paula says. You never even leave the neighbourhood.

Halfway up the mountain, I say, the sky changes colour from blue to black, and half an hour later it starts to snow. It snows so heavily that seven adults and twelve or thirteen kids get snowed into a space under a crag on Ben Wyvis. It's before the days of mobile phones. There's no way of letting anyone know where we are. It's freezing. We huddle together, then the adults huddle the kids inside a circle of their bodies. It's afternoon. It gets dark. It doesn't stop snowing. All there is is snow in the dark, and more snow, and dark at the back of it, snow for miles of empty sky, and a lot of swearing from my father, he's dead now, and the man from across the road, he's dead now too, I think, threatening to murder Mr Fenimore, and my mother who'd worn shoes with heels on to go up a mountain in, my mother, she'd never even been on a hike before never mind anywhere near a mountain, cursing herself, and a bit of arguing about who should go for help, and Mrs Fenimore crying, and Mr Fenimore counting heads every five minutes, before he sets off into the white dark to bring help back.

Oh God, Tom says. Does he die?

It ends happily, Paula says. Doesn't it?

Mr Fenimore is lost on the hill till the next day, when the rescue services pick him up, I say. He's in hospital for a week. We're all already home by then. We all get picked up about an hour later by three men in a helicopter. The father of a girl called Jenny McKenzie, in the year above me at school, has picked up the bad forecast on the radio and phoned the rescue services and told them where we went. They keep four of us in hospital overnight, including me. It's a laugh. We're all fine. But the thing is, we get back to town, back home, and – there's no snow anywhere. None. It's all just like normal, grey pavements and tarmac and roofs, like none of it happened.

Then what? Tom says.

What happened about the Fenimores? Paula says.

How was that a happy Christmas? Tom says.

I had no idea what happened to the Fenimores, I realised, sitting there by myself in the warmed-up seat in my car in a near-empty car park miles from home. I could remember her sad face. I could remember his open, naive brow, his forward slant when he walked down the school corridor or up the makings of a path at the foot of the ben. They were only there for that year, maybe. They moved away. The judo club stopped. A home economics teacher took over the cookery club. People stopped talking about them like they were the local joke pretty soon. Where were those people, the hopeful man and his sad helpful love; where were the Fenimores tonight, nearly thirty years later? Were they warm in a house, well into their middle-age? Were they still the Fenimores?

From here in my car I could see the frosty roofs on the village terrace below, down at the bottom of the slope. I looked the other way and saw, through the side window of the pub, the man and the barmaid.

The man had his back to the bar. He was holding a near-empty glass, staring ahead into space. The barmaid was leaning on her elbow. She was staring in the opposite direction. They stayed like that, unmoving, like figures in a painting, the whole time I watched.

The barmaid was called Paula. I had no idea what the man's name was. Good, because I didn't want to know. I was just a stranger who ordered supper and didn't eat it. I was long gone, as far as they knew, on the road out of here in the dark.

I put my hand on the ignition key, whisky or no whisky.

But if I went back inside, I could eat. And if I went back inside, if I was simply there, those two people would speak to each other again, they'd be able to, even if I was just sitting reading my paper or eating my supper ignoring them.

I looked down at the roofs of the houses sheened with the fierce frost, like a row of faraway houses in the kind of story we tell ourselves about winter and its chancy gifts.

I opened the car door and got out. I locked it, though I probably didn't need to, and I went back into the pub.

the third person

All short stories long.

This one is about two people who have just gone to bed together for the first time. It's autumn. They met in the summer. Since they met they've been working up to this with a sense of unavoidability; less a courtship, more as if they've found themselves in a very small room, like a box room, a room small enough to feel overcrowded with two people in it, and this room also has a grand piano in it. It doesn't matter where they've been or what they've been doing – meeting each other by chance in the street, walking down the road, going to a cinema, sitting at a table in a pub – it's as if they're in a tiny room and in there with them, massive, ever-present as an old-fashioned chaperone, awkward and glossy and unmentionable as a coffin, the grand piano. To move at all in this room means having to squeeze into the narrow space between the wall and the side of the piano. The inside of it, under the lid, is a structure of wires and hammers a bit like the underframe of a bed or a harp that's been laid on its side.

They've done it, they've shrugged themselves out of their shy clothes at last, they've slipped in under the covers of a small double bed, they're holding each other in nothing but skin. One of them even has a quite bad cold and the other doesn't care. Ah, love. Outside, the trees are quiet. The light is coming down. It's five in the evening. But enough about them. It's spring. It's morning. In the trees the birds are singing like crazy. A woman living in a street of terraced houses, a street on which so many cars are parked that it makes driving the fortnightly refuse-collector truck down it quite difficult, has just hit one of the dustmen who routinely empty the wheelie bins every second Tuesday morning over the head with a garden spade.

The man is on the ground. He's bleeding from the forehead. He is looking bewildered. He holds up his hand and looks at the blood on it. He puts it back up to his forehead again.

The woman is leaning on the spade as if her

spade's blade, on the pavement, is a couple of inches into earth and she's simply tidying her garden and has paused to take stock of what work she's done. She looks about sixty. She looks quite well-to-do. She looks too old, too proper, too well dressed, to have done what she's just done. Round her, round him now, the man's work colleagues off the truck are gathered in a tableau, open-mouthed, between laughter and anger. The driver of the truck is hanging out of the front cabin, one foot on the step, the door swinging open behind him. All the men are wearing the same green council overalls. It's summer. It's evening. The trees are different here. On one of the back streets of a small Mediterranean resort two women are eating at a restaurant whose tables are wooden and rickety. The table they're at shifts its weight between them every time one or other of them cuts something up on her plate. The street is a slope; one of the women is a lot higher up on its slant than the other, even though she's just two feet away.

The women are bright pink from four days of too much sun. The one on the up slope is still exclaiming over the way that tomatoes taste so different here, the way that everything tastes so different here. Everything tastes of sun. The other, on the down slope, is beginning to worry about what she'll do when she gets bored with eating Greek salad, since there's nothing else she likes the look of on this menu but there's no other restaurant in the tiny resort that she likes the look of, not really, and it was touch and go about whether they'd be able to get a table at this one again tonight.

Gypsy children go up and down the street just like on each of the other evenings, but tonight the braying noise of the little squeezeboxes they use for begging is almost drowned out by the Americans. The Americans are off-duty troops. They are sly looking and shy looking, polite looking and hangdog looking and only just school-leaving-age looking; they look so young and so raw that it's really near-criminal. The women have gathered, from overhearing them talk, that they're here en masse on a working holiday to accustom them to sun and heat before they're shipped to the Gulf. When the women exclaimed to the waiter about the number of people in the restaurant tonight, this is what he told them.

Three ships, many thousand troops, arrive on the resort's outer harbour. So the bars on the outskirts unwrap the big boots this morning and put them on the tables and then everybody knows what is happening, and the big boots go through the town like a fire. And then the soldiers in two or three days go away and the boots are wrapped in the paper again until the next ships.

The waiter shrugged. The women nodded and looked interested. When the waiter went, they made faces at each other to let each other know that neither had understood what he was talking about.

Now a small child is standing next to their table. She is working the tables at this restaurant with a boy of about ten who plays the same perfect Italian-sounding cliché over and over on his child-sized squeezebox. He looks businesslike and disinterested as he holds his hand out at the end of each riff at table after table. The girl standing pressed up against the women's table is dark, very pretty, very young, maybe only five or six years old. She says something they don't understand. The woman on the down slope shakes her head and waves at the girl to go away. The woman on the up slope picks their Rough Guide Phrasebook up off the table. She flicks through it. Ya soo, she says while she does. The child smiles. She speaks in shy English. Give me money, the smiling child says. She says it seductively, almost under her breath. The woman has found the page she wants.

Pos se leneh? the woman says.

Money, the child says.

She presses up against the woman's leg and puts her small hand on the woman's arm. The hand is very brown from sun. Poso khronon iseh? the woman says, then tells the other woman, I'm asking her how old she is.

It's when they go to pay the bill that the woman on the up slope will find out that the wad of euros she had, folded deep down in her pocket, isn't in her pocket anymore.

It isn't in any of her other pockets.

Then they'll remember the child backing off and calling to the squeezebox boy, then both disappearing in among the hundreds of off-duty soldiers.

It was a piece of perfect thievery, a piece of artistry so good that the doing of it was invisible. All the way back to the hotel that night the down-slope woman, the one who hasn't had her money stolen and who has had to pay for supper, will be annoyed with herself that she has witnessed such a perfect act of thievery and somehow not actually seen it happen. She will berate herself for this not-seeing. She will feel, as they walk back to their hotel, the sheer unfairness of her own life again as the up-slope woman, walking next to her, argues on her mobile the whole way back at ten o'clock at night with the 24-hour desk at her travel insurance company. Neither will notice that the bars and pubs they both walk past along the tourist harbourfront are surreal with outsized beer-glasses, glasses a foot and a half high; on all their counters, all their outside tables, beer-glasses shaped like seven-league boots, with see-through straps and buckles and see-through leather flaps sculpted in the glass they're made of. It's winter. The trees are bare. A woman and a man have gone to see a production of a play at a theatre. He bought the tickets months back, in the summer. She likes this kind of thing. But their time as a couple is nearly up, the man knows, because he has seen how the woman has begun to despise him, he saw it on Saturday evening, when he was cutting courgettes into strips for a stir-fry, he saw it cross her face. He feels that the end of their love must be something to do with the way he cuts vegetables. He doesn't know what else to blame. It has made him uneasy in his own kitchen, and tonight when they ate out at a restaurant near the theatre he could touch nothing green on his plate.

On the stage a woman has disguised herself to go and meet her lover in a wood; her lover has been banished by her father, the king. The woods thicken. The plot goes crazy. She takes what she thinks is a medicine and falls into a sleep so deep that it looks like death. Her new-found friends in the wood put her in a tomb, believing she's dead. They sing a song above the body. The song is about death being a place of no more fear. When he hears this song the man in the audience starts to cry. He can't help it. The song is very moving. She takes his hand. She holds it. He stops crying.

He doesn't dare open his eyes in case the opening of his eyes will mean she will let go of his hand. All round him, in the dark of his own shut eyes and then in the sudden lights-up of the theatre, in the light which comes as suddenly through his shut eyelids as it would were his eyes open, as if eyelids are no protection at all, there's sudden applause. Interval. The play is half over. It's summer. The nights are long and light. Right now it's the brief summer dark of early morning, just before the light comes up. A young woman wakes up next to her new lover and sees someone sitting there in the dark at the end of the bed. It is an old woman moving her hands, knitting. The young woman shakes her lover gently. She doesn't dare say anything out loud in case the old woman is startled. But her lover is fast asleep.

The next day at breakfast she describes the figure to her lover. It sounds like my mother, her lover says. Her lover's mother has apparently been dead for a decade. Was she singing? her lover asks. Yes, the young woman says, she was, she definitely was. What was she singing? the lover asks. I don't know, she says, but it had a bit in it that sounded like this.

She sings a tune, making it up as she goes along. She tries to make it sound like it could be a real tune. It is a mix of the Londonderry Air and a song from a record her own mother used to play when she was small.

No, I don't think I know it, her lover says. Sing it again.

The young woman sings a bit of a tune again but it's not the same as the first time because she can't remember what she's just sung. She sees her lover frowning. She sings a made-up tune again. She tries to make it the kind of tune she imagines the mother of her lover would sing.

No, that's definitely not my mother, her lover says. Her lover puts a cup down on a saucer so decisively that the young woman knows the matter is closed. The young woman is disappointed. She now really wants the figure at the end of the bed to have been the lover's dead mother. What if it *was* your mother and she was just singing a tune you don't happen to know? she says. There must be *some* tunes your mother knew that you don't know. It's summer, but it's cold, really noticeably cold. Tonight it's almost down to freezing. A man in a restaurant is telling his friend about the death of a soldier. The soldier who has died was ten years younger than the man and was a small boy in the same neighbourhood all through the man's adolescence. He died in a roadside incident, is what it says in the papers. The man is holding a folded newspaper. Inside on page 5 there is a report about the death of a soldier, but because the soldier's family has asked for privacy, there are no names, though everybody in the neighbourhood knows who the articles in the papers are about. *He died in the heroic fight,* it says. What heroic fight? the man says. All round them people are talking and laughing. I helped him build a go-cart, the man says. I nailed an old steering-wheel on to it for him and tied wire to the wheels so it would steer. I was seventeen. Then, when he was older, we used to just ignore each other. If we saw each other in the street, I mean. The man's friend shakes his head. He doesn't know what to say. It's so strange, he says. It's so. It's. It's spring. It's an early evening in April, the first mild evening of spring. A man is out on his flat roof with a hosepipe, aiming a jet of water at a small black and white cat. When the water hits the cat, the cat jumps in the air and runs a little, and then turns and stops and looks at the man.

Go on, the man shouts. He waves his hand in

the air. The cat doesn't move. The man aims the hose again. He hits the cat. The cat jumps in astonishment again, takes a few steps, then stops and turns to look back at the man with its wide stupid cat eyes.

Aw, a voice says.

It is quite a high voice.

The man checks all round him at the roofs and gardens of the other houses but he can't see anyone.

Go on, he shouts at the cat again. He stamps on the roof.

When he's chased the cat right down the back lane with the water, the man crosses the roof, gathering in the hose. He climbs in his window and turns to shake the nozzle outside. That's when he sees the small boy, or maybe it's a girl, edging down out of one of the sycamore trees at the back of the houses.

The boy or girl has what looks like a book, or maybe a cardboard packet, under one arm. Biscuits? The man watches him or her negotiate a safe way down from quite high up in the trees, moving the packet from under one arm to under the other, careful from branch to branch until he or she is within reach of the roof of the shed in the garden below. Then the boy or girl slides downwards and out of view.

That night the man can't sleep. He turns in his bed. He sits up.

A child believes I am cruel, he is thinking to himself.

The next morning he is almost late for work, not just because he woke late, but because he goes and stands out on the roof for several minutes then leaves home later than usual. That evening he takes a taxi, but though he's home half an hour early and goes straight out on to the roof, it's raining, and it's noticeably cold, much colder than yesterday.

There's no way a child would climb a tree in such weather. The tree would be too slippery. There'd be no point in sitting in a tree in the rain.

The leaves are nearly out on these trees. It'll soon be summer. The ends of their branches against the grey sky look like they're swollen, or lit, or like they've been painted with luminous paint.

It doesn't look like it will brighten. It doesn't look like anything is going to happen tonight.

He decides he'll wait out there on the roof for a little while longer, just in case.

The third person is another pair of eyes. The third person is a presentiment of God. The third person is a way to tell the story. The third person is a revitalisation of the dead.

It's a theatre of living people. It's a miniature innocent thief. It's thousands of boots that are made out of glass. It's a total mystery.

It's a weapon that's shaped like a tool.

It comes out of nowhere. It just happens.

It's a box for the endless music that's there between people, waiting to be played.

fidelio and bess

A young woman is ironing in a kitchen in a prison. But she's not a prisoner, no. Her father's the chief gaoler; she just lives here. A young man comes into the kitchen and tells her he's decided that he and she are going to marry. I've chosen you, he says. She is desultory with him. She suggests to the audience that he's a bit of a fool. Then she sings a song to herself. It's Fidelio I've chosen, it's Fidelio I'm in love with, she sings. It's Fidelio who's in love with me. It's Fidelio I want to wake up next to every morning.

Her father comes home. Then, a moment later, so does Fidelio himself, who looks suspiciously like a girl dressed as a boy, and who happens to be wreathed in chains. Not that Fidelio's a prisoner, no. Apparently the chains have been being repaired by a blacksmith (whom we never see), and Fidelio, the girl's father's assistant, has brought the mended chains back to the gaol.

But it seems that Fidelio isn't much interested in marrying the boss's daughter. Fidelio, instead, is unnaturally keen to meet a mysterious prisoner who's being kept in the deepest, darkest underground cell in the prison. This particular prisoner has been down there for two years and is receiving almost no food or water any more. This is on the prison governor's orders; the prison governor wants him starved to death. He's clearly a man who's done great wrong, Fidelio says, fishing for information – or made great enemies, which is pretty much the same thing, the gaoler says, leaning magnanimously back in his kitchen chair. Money, he says. It's the answer to everything. The girl looks at Fidelio. Don't let *him* see that dying prisoner, the girl says. He couldn't stand it, he's just a boy, he's such a gentle boy. Don't subject him to such a cruel sight. On the contrary, Fidelio says. Let me see him. I'm brave enough and I'm strong enough.

But then the prison governor announces to the gaoler, in private, that he has just decided to have this prisoner killed. *I'm* not murdering him, the gaoler says when the governor tells him to. Okay, I'll do it myself, the prison governor says. I'll take pleasure in it. And I'll give you a bag of gold if you go and dig a grave for him in the old well down there in his cell.

It's agreed. In the next Act the gaoler will take the boy Fidelio down to the deep dungeon and they'll dig the grave for the man who, we've begun to gather, is Fidelio's imprisoned husband. Meanwhile, as the First Act draws to a close, Fidelio has somehow managed to get all the other prisoners in the place released out of the dark of their cells into the weak spring sun in the prison yard for a little while.

They stagger out into the light. They stand about, ragged, dazed, heartbreakingly hopeful. They're like a false resurrection. They look up at the sunlight. Summertime, they sing, and the living is easy. Fish are jumping and the cotton is high.

Then they all look at each other in amazement.

Fidelio looks bewildered.

The gaoler shakes his head.

The conductor's baton droops.

The orchestra in the pit stops playing. Instruments pause in mid-air.

The girl who was doing the ironing at the beginning is singing too. She's really good. She shrugs at her father as if she can't help it, can't do anything about it. Your daddy's rich, she sings, and your mammy's good-looking.

Then a man arrives in a cart pulled by a goat. He stops the cart in the middle of the stage. Everybody crowds round him. He's black. He's the only black person on the stage. He looks very poor and at the same time very impressive. When the song finishes he gets out of the cart. He walks across the stage. He's got a limp. It's quite a bad limp. He tells them all that he's looking for Bess. Where is she? He's heard she's here. He's not going to stop looking for her until he finds her. He glances at the gaoler; he regards Fidelio gravely for a moment. He nods to the girl. He approaches a group of prisoners. Is this New York? he says. Is she here?

Yeah, but, you say. Come on. I mean.

But what? I say.

You can't, you say.

Can't what? I say.

Culture's fixed, you say. That's why it's culture. That's how it gets to be art. That's how it works. That's why it works. You can't just change it. You can't just alter it when you want or because you want. You can't just revise things for your own pleasure or whatever.

Actually I can do anything I like, I say.

Yeah, but you can't revise Fidelio, you say. No one can.

Fidelio's all about revision, I say. Beethoven

revised Fidelio several times. Three different versions. Four different overtures.

You know what I mean. No one can just, as it were, interject Porgy into Fidelio, you say.

Oh, *as it were*, I say.

You don't say anything. You stare straight out, ahead, through the windscreen.

Okay. I know what you mean, I say.

You start humming faintly, under your own breath.

But I don't think interject is quite the right word to use there, I say.

I say this because I know there's nothing that annoys you more than thinking you've used a word wrongly. You snort down your nose.

Yes it is, you say.

I don't think it's quite the right usage, I say.

It is, you say. Anyway, I didn't say interject. I said inject.

I lean forward and switch the radio on. I keep pressing the channel button until I hear something I recognise.

It's fine for you to do that, you say, but if you're going to, can you at least, before we get out of the car, return it to the channel to which it was originally tuned?

I settle on some channel or other, I've no idea what.

Which channel was it on? you say.

Radio 4, I say.

Are you sure? you say.

Or 3, I say.

Which? you say.

I don't know, I say.

You sigh.

Gilbert O'Sullivan is singing the song about the people who are hurrying to the register office to get married. *Very shortly now there's going to be an answer from you. Then one from me.* I sing along. You sigh out loud again. The sigh lifts the hair of your fringe slightly from your forehead.

You're so pretty when you sigh like that.

When we arrive at the car park you reach over to my side of the radio and keep the little button pressed in until the radio hits the voices of a comedy programme where celebrities have one minute exactly to talk about a subject, with no repetitions. If they repeat themselves, they're penalized. An audience is killing itself laughing.

When you're sure it's Radio 4, you switch the radio off.

We are doomed as a couple. We are as categorically doomed as when Clara in Porgy and Bess says: *Jake, you ain't plannin' to take de Sea Gull to de Blackfish Banks, is you? It's time for de*

September storms. No, the Sea Gull, a fictional boat, moored safe and ruined both at once in its own eternal bay, is less doomed than we are. We're as doomed as the Cutty Sark itself, tall, elegant, real, mundanely gathering the London sky round its masts and making it wondrous, extraordinary, for the people coming up out of the underground train station in the evening, the ship-of-history gracious against the sky for all the people who see it and all the people who don't even notice it any more because they're so used to seeing it, and just two months to go before there'll be nothing left of it but a burnt-out hull, a scoop of scorched plankwork.

We are doomed on land and doomed on sea, you and me; as doomed holding on to each other's arms on the underground as we are arguing about culture in your partner's car; as doomed in a bar sitting across from each other or side by side at the cinema or the opera or the theatre; as doomed as we are when we're pressed into each other in the various beds in the various near-identical rooms we go to, to have the sex that your partner doesn't know about us having. Of all the dooms I ever thought I might come to I never reckoned on middle-classness. You and me, holding hands below the seats at Fidelio, an opera you've already seen, already taken your partner to;

and it all started so anarchically, so happily, all heady public kissing in King's Cross station. *Mir ist so wunderbar.* That's me in the £120-a-night bed, and you through in the bathroom, thoroughly cleaning your teeth.

I've read in the sleeve notes for the version of Fidelio I have on CD that at an early point in the opera, when all four people, the girl, the thwarted young man, the woman dressed as a boy and the gaoler, are singing about happiness and everybody is misunderstanding everybody else and believing a different version of things to be true, that this is where 'backstairs chat turns into the music of the angels'. *How wonderful it is to me. Something's got my heart in its grip. He loves me, it's clear. I'm going to be happy.* Except, wunderbar here doesn't mean the usual simple wonderful. It means full of wonder, strange. *How strange it is to me.* I wish I could remember her name, the ironing girl who loves Fidelio, the light-comedy act-opener, the girl for whom there's no real end to it, the girl who has to accept – with nothing more than an alas, which pretty soon modulates into the same song everyone else is singing – what happens when the boy Fidelio is suddenly revealed as the wife Leonore, and everybody stands round her in awe at her wifely faithfulness, her profound self-sacrifice. *O namenlose.*

Which is worse to her, the ironing girl? That Fidelio is really Leonore, a woman, not the boy she thought he was? Or that her beloved Fidelio is someone else's wife, after all, and so, in this opera about the sacredness of married love, will never, ever be hers?

Oh my Leonore, Florestan, the husband, the freed prisoner, says to Fidelio after she's unearthed him, after she's flung herself between him and certain death, between him and the drawn blade of the prison governor. Point of catharsis. Point of truth. After she does this, everything in the whole world changes for the better.

Oh my Leonore, what have you done for me?

Nothing, nothing, my Florestan, she answers.

Lucky for her she had a gun on her, that's what I say, otherwise they'd both be dead.

Oh, I got plenty o' nuttin. And nuttin's plenty fo' me.

It's famously unresolved, you know, I say. Even though its ending seems so celebratory, so C-major, so huge and comforting and sure, there's still a sense, at the back of it all, that lots of things haven't been resolved. Look at the ironing girl, for instance. She's not resolved, is she? Beethoven called it his 'child of sorrow'. He never wrote another opera after it.

Half a year ago you'd never heard of Fidelio, you say.

Klemperer conducted it at two really extraordinarily different times in history, I say.

I am flicking through the little book that comes with the version of Fidelio you've just given me. The new CD is one of my Christmas presents. Christmas is in ten days' time. We have just opened our Christmas presents, in a bedroom in a Novotel. I bought you a really nice French-looking jumper, with buttons at one side of the neck. I know that you'll probably drop it in a litter bin on your way home.

Imagine, I say. Imagine conducting it in 1915 in the middle of the First World War. Then imagine the strangeness of conducting it in the 1960s, when every single scene must have reminded people of the different thing it meant, for a German conductor, the story of all the people starved and tyranted, buried alive, for being themselves, for saying the truth, for standing up to the status quo.

Tyranted's not a word, you say in my ear.

You say it lovingly. You are holding me in your arms. We are both naked. You are warm behind me. You make my back feel blessed, the way you are holding me. I can feel the curve of your breasts at each of my shoulder blades.

Imagine all the things that Florestan must have meant, then, I say, to those people, in that audience in 1915, then 1961.

It's an opera, you say. It's nothing to do with history.

Yes, but it is, I say. It's post-Napoleonic. That's obvious. Imagine what it meant to its audience in 1814. Imagine watching the same moment in this opera at different times in history. Take the moment when Fidelio asks whether she can give the prisoner a piece of old bread. It's the question of whether one starving man can have a piece of mercy. All the millions of war dead are in it there, crowding behind that one man. And the buried, unearthed truth. And the new day dawning, and all the old ghosts coming out of the ground.

Uh huh, you say.

What if Fidelio had been written by Mozart? I say.

It wasn't, you say.

The knockabout there'd have been with Fidelio in her boy's clothes, I say. The swagger Mozart would have given Rocco. The good joke the girl who's ironing at the start would have become, and the boy too, who thinks he can just marry her because he's made up his mind he wants to.

You yawn.

Though there's something really interesting in

the way Beethoven doesn't force those characters to be funny, I say. The ironing girl, what's her name? There's something humane in the way they're not just, you know, played for laughs.

You kiss the back of my neck. You use your teeth on my shoulder. It's allowed, you biting me. I quite like to be gently bitten. I'm not allowed to bite you, though, in case it marks you.

I still have no idea whether you like being gently bitten or not.

Not long after we'd met, when I said I'd never heard much, didn't know much about Beethoven, you played me some on your iPod. When I said I thought it sounded like Jane Austen crossed with Daniel Libeskind, you looked bemused, like I was a clever child. When I said that what I meant was that it was like different kinds of architecture, as if a classically eighteenth-century room had suddenly morphed into a postmodern annexe, you shook your head and kissed me to make me stop talking. I closed my eyes into the kiss. I love your kiss. Everything's sorted, and obvious, and understood, and civilised, your kiss says. It's a shut-eye lie, I know it is, because the music I didn't know before I knew you makes me open my eyes in a place of no sentimentality, where light itself is a kind of shadow, where everything is fragment-slanted. A couple of months later, when I said I thought you could hear the whole of history in it, all history's grandnesses and sadnesses, you'd looked a bit annoyed. You'd taken the iPod off my knee and disconnected its headphones from their socket. When I'd removed the dead headphones from my ears you'd rolled them up carefully and tucked them into the special little carrying-case you keep them in. You'd said you were getting a migraine. Impatience had crossed your face so firmly that I had known, in that instant, that now we were actually a kind of married, and that our marriedness was probably making your real relationship more palatable.

Sometimes a marriage needs three hearts beating as one.

I've met your partner. She's nice. I can tell she's quite a nice person. She knows who I am but she doesn't know who I am. Her clothes smell overwhelmingly of the same washing powder as yours.

Ten days before Christmas, smelling of sex in a rented bed, with half an hour to go before you have to get the half past ten train home, I hold the new Fidelio in my hands. I think of the ironing girl, holding up the useless power of her own huge love to Fidelio in the First Act like a chunk of dead stone she thinks is full of magic. I think of Fidelio herself, insufferably righteous. I think about how she makes her first entrance laden with chains that aren't actually binding her to anything.

I open the plastic box and I take out one of the shiny discs. I hold it up in front of us and we look at our reflection, our two heads together, in the spectrum-split plastic of the first half of the opera.

So is marriage a matter of chains? I say.

Eh? you say.

Or a matter of the kind of faithfulness that brings dead things back to life? I say.

I have absolutely no idea what you're talking about, you say.

I lean my head back on your collarbone and turn it so that my mouth touches the top of your arm. I feel with my teeth the front of your shoulder.

Don't bite me, you say.

Marzelline. That's her name.

Gershwin wrote six prayers to be sung simultaneously, for the storm scene in Porgy and Bess. As an opera, Porgy and Bess did comparatively badly at the box office. So did the early versions of Fidelio; it wasn't till 1814 that audiences were ready to acclaim it. At the end of one, all the prisoners are free and all the self-delusion about love is irrelevant. At the end of the other, there's nothing to do but go off round the world, on one good leg and one ruined leg, in search of the lost beloved. I guess you got me fo' keeps, Porgy, Bess says, before she's gone, gone, gone, gone, gone, gone, gone.

Will I dress as a boy and stand outside your house, all its windows lit for your Christmas party, its music filtering out into the dark? Will I stand in the dark and take a pick or a spade to the hard surface of the turf of your midwinter back lawn? Will I dig till I'm covered in dust and earth, till I uncover the whole truth, the house of dust under the ground? Will I shake the soil off the long iron chain fixed to the slab of rock deep in the earth beneath the pretty lavenders, the annuals and perennials of your suburban garden?

It is Saturday night. It is summertime on a quiet hot street in a port town. A man plays a sleepy lament on a piano. Some men play dice. A woman married to a fisherman is rocking a baby to sleep. Her husband takes the baby out of her arms and sings it his own version of a lullaby. A woman is a some time thing, he sings. The baby cries. Everybody laughs.

Porgy arrives home. He's a cripple; he rides in a

cart pulled by a goat. He goes to join in the dice game. A man arrives with a woman in tow; the man is Crown and the woman is Bess. His job is the unloading and loading of cargo from ships. Her job is to be his, and to keep herself happy on happy dust, drugs. These dice, Porgy says shaking them, are my morning and my evening stars. An' just you watch 'em rise and shine for this poor beggar.

But Crown is high on drink and dust. When he loses at dice he starts a fight. He kills someone with a cotton hook. Get out of here, Bess tells him, the police will be here any minute. At the mention of the police, everybody on the street disappears except the dead man, the dead man's mourning wife, and Bess, who finds all the doors of all the houses shut against her.

Then, unexpectedly, one door opens. It's the door of Porgy, the cripple. She's about to go in, but at the last moment she doesn't. She turns and looks at the side of the stage instead. Everything on stage stops, holds its breath.

The orchestra stops.

A white girl has entered from the wings. She is standing, lost-looking, over by the edge of the set.

Bess stares at her. Porgy, still at his door, stares at her. Serena, the dead man's wife, stares at her. The dead man, Robbins, opens his eyes and puts his head up and stares at her.

The doors of the other houses on the set open; the windows open. All the other residents of Catfish Row look out. They come out of the houses. They're sweating, from the heat under the stage-lights, under the hot summer night. They stand at a distance, their sweat glistening, their eyes on the white girl with the iron in her hand.

The girl starts to sing.

A brother has come to seek her brothers, she sings. To help them if she can with all her heart.

Everybody on stage looks to Porgy, the cripple. He looks to Bess, who shrugs, then nods.

Porgy nods too. He opens his door wider.

the history of history

My mother was sitting on the top stair with her arm round the neck of the dog, whose front paws were up on her knees. She was reading a Georgette Heyer book. There was no tea on. There was no sign of anything to do with tea in the kitchen. My father would be home in an hour.

I stood at the foot of the stairs for a while. The dog looked down at me, wagged her tail. My mother turned a page and yawned. I slung my schoolbag strap round the knob of the banister, opened the bag, took my books and pencil case out and went through to the living room. I had homework for tomorrow. *Write a newspaper report of the death of Mary Queen of Scots. Translate pages 31–33 of La Symphonie Pastorale by André Gide.* I hated La Symphonie Pastorale.

It was a load of sentimental rubbish about a blind girl. I called my father at his work from the living-room phone. I lifted the receiver carefully so the hall phone wouldn't make the little ting that would give away that someone was on the other phone.

You'll need to bring chips, I said.

I can hear you, my mother called down the stairs. If you're telling him to bring chips, tell him I want a haddock.

She wants a haddock, I said.

Couldn't you put something in the oven? my father said. We've had chips three times this week.

Actually I can't put something in the oven because there's nothing in the house, I said over by the door, loud enough for her to hear me.

There's people in the house, not nothing, my mother called down. And there's a dog. That's not nothing, people and a dog.

I can't hear you, I said to my father. She's shouting stuff.

I hung up and went back to the table and wrote up what we'd taken notes on in double history.

A hush came over the crowd as the doomed queen was led to the place of execution. She was dressed in black satin and velvet and she undressed, saying, 'I have never put off my clothes before in front of such a company.' Underneath her clothes she was wearing red clothes, and her handmaidens then put long red sleeves on her arms and pinned them to her underclothes. She smiled and prayed and said goodbye to those who had served her all her life. There was much crying in the room. Her handmaidens fastened a white cloth across her eyes and she stumbled forward to lay her head on the block. In fact she also put her hands on the block, but luckily someone noticed at the last minute or these would also have been cut off as well as her head. Then the executioner tried to cut her head off, but the first time he missed and only cut her head a bit open. The execution was properly executed the second time and when the executioner held her head up it fell out of his hands and all that was left in his hands was a wig, and the beautiful queen was revealed to everybody as an old lady with very short grey hair. Legend has it that her lips were still moving many minutes after her head was cut off and that her little dog, which was of the breed of Skye Terrier, hid in among her skirts and then curled itself round the place between her shoulders where her head had been, and then it later died as well, of sorrow.

It was only a first draft. The idea was that we were meant to make it as much like a real newspaper report as possible. I went through it again and decided what was important and what wasn't, if it was for a newspaper, and gave it suitable headings and columns.

VERY FASHIONABLE
The doomed queen was led
to the place of execution. A
hush came over the crowd
when it saw her. She was
dressed very fashionably in
black satin and velvet.
Many ladies nodded at her
fashion taste.

EMBARRASSING
The crowd held its breath while
she took off nearly all her
clothes. All the people there
could nearly see what she
would look like with no clothes
on. It was embarrassing. She
was wearing bright red
underwear. Goodbye! she said
to everyone. She smiled a
queenly smile. The crowd burst
into tears. She was the People's
Queen. Her hand-maidens fixed
a white cloth on her eyes.

WEARING A WIG

When she came forward to
the block, she stumbled. The
crowd all went oooh! aaah!
After two swipes of the axe,
she was unfortunately dead.
The executioner picked up her
head. That's when it was
revealed to everyone that she
had grey hair and wore a wig
and was not at all as beautiful
as people had thought, but
much older in actuality.

NOBLE BREED

Legend has it that she spoke for
a long time after being dead,
though nobody has reported
what it was she actually said.
We at the DAILY NEWS
believe she probably said 'I am
dead. Do not grieve for me.
Please make sure my dog is fed
properly after my demise.' Her
dog, a Skye Terrier, which is a
noble breed, would not leave
her side even when she was
dead. Then it would not leave

the place where her head once
was. Then it died too. And
that was the sad end of the
noble breed herself, the
Scottish queen of Scots, and
also of her dog.

I heard something clattering on the stairs.

Christ almighty I hate these fucking books, my
mother was shouting. They're full of shit. I'm
never going to read a single one of these again in
my life.

She must have thrown the book down the stairs.
That must have been what had made the clattering
noise. Either that or she'd thrown the dog.

I had never heard her use language like that
before.

I very much disapproved.

My mother's gone mad, I told my friend Sandra
next day at school.

Mine too, Sandra said. All she does is make
things and put them in Tupperware boxes in the
freezer. It's because the people next door got a
freezer and then my dad got us one, a really huge
one in the garage and it's like she can't bear to
think of it having any space left in it so she's busy
freezing things.

No, I mean really mad, I said, not just normal mad. She won't cook anything. She says I'm to call her by her real name.

What's she mean, real name? Sandra said.

Margaret, I said. She keeps saying that's the name she was born with. She won't answer to anything other than that anymore. I mean, I can't call her, like, Margaret. I can't say, I'll be back at ten, Margaret, I'm going out with Roddy. I can't say, I'm home, Margaret, when I get home after school. It sounds stupid.

Yeah, Sandra said. Right.

She laughed a laugh that wasn't really a laugh, like I'd told her a joke she didn't understand.

It started last month, I said. She began to say things like, I'm a person, and all that kind of thing. Then she was just, like, watching TV a couple of weeks ago, that programme The Good Life, it was something about the posh one singing in a choir. And she stood up and said, I am no longer your wife, to my dad, and I am no longer your mother, to me. Then she went out in the car and we didn't know where she'd gone, and when she came back it was two in the morning and we thought it would be okay, but the next day she was still saying the stuff.

Oh, Sandra said.

Sandra was my best friend, but she was walking a little further away from me. She was listening but she was looking not at me but at the ground, as though something baffling was walking two feet ahead of her.

Worst fucking thing is, she's started swearing now, I said.

But it was as if I'd told my best friend I was gay, or something astonishing like that, and made her feel embarrassed because of me.

Oh yeah, by the way, she said. I can't walk home at four o'clock today. I've got to go to town with my mum.

If it was me, imagine, I'd be having to go to town with someone called Margaret, I said. I'd be saying, I can't walk home with you because I've got to go to town with Margaret. And you'd be like, who's Margaret?

Yeah, she said. Ha ha.

What's your mum's real name anyway? I said.

Eh, it's Shona, she said. Bye.

Imagine that, I called after her. Imagine you're going into town with Shona, not your mother at all.

She went round the corner out of earshot without looking back. We went our separate ways to our separate classes; I'd taken languages and history, she'd taken geography and science.

When I got home my mother had cut down the hedge at the end of the garden, which meant there was nothing between our garden and the train-line. There was no fence at the end of the garden at all any more. There was no sign of the dog.

Look, my mother said. Now we can see so much further.

Now the people on the platform can see right into our house, I said. The train people won't be pleased with you doing that.

She sat down on the grass among the strands of hedge.

You used to be so much more of an independent thinker, she said to me.

I'm running out of clean clothes, I said. I've almost nothing left to wear that doesn't need washed. I don't know how to work the machine. Neither does Dad.

You'll manage, she said.

She sighed. She looked up. She said, look at that!

I looked, but it was only a blackbird in a tree. I sighed too.

What's for tea? I said.

You're like me, she said. You're tenacious.

I'm nothing like you, I said.

I turned and went back towards the house to phone my father.

You'll be all right, she called after me.

No I won't, I shouted back over my own shoulder.

no exit

I'm in bed. It's three a.m. I'm wide awake. I turn on to my side. I turn on to my back again. Earlier tonight I was at the cinema watching a film and I saw the woman who'd been sitting a couple of seats along from me get up midway through it and go down the stairs in the dark. She pushed the bar down on the fire exit door, the one over on the left hand side of the big screen. The door swung shut behind her, and I knew, because I know a little about the building, that she'd gone out through the illegal fire exit, the one that actually leads nowhere. Behind that door is nothing but a flight of stairs downwards and two locked doors.

I looked around me at all the other people watching the film. It was a new British film about the relationship between the East and the West.

Right then on the screen a man with a moustache was threatening a spiky-haired man with a kitchen knife.

I looked down at the fire exit doors again. The sign above was lit up, with the word EXIT on it and the small green shape of a running man. But the doors were shut, and it was as if nobody had ever gone through them.

I wondered if anyone else sitting here with me knew there was no way out of there, and no way back through after the doors had sealed shut on you. I wondered whether it was only me in the whole audience who knew. I told myself that if she wasn't back in her seat at the end of the film, I'd tell whoever it was she'd come to the cinema with that I'd seen where she went. We would go down the stairs and open the door and she'd probably be standing there patiently on the other side of it waiting for someone to let her back into the auditorium.

I couldn't concentrate on the film.

Maybe the woman had thought it was the way to the toilet. Or, more hopefully, maybe she worked at the cinema. Probably she'd gone in there on purpose. Probably she had a key to one of the locked doors in there.

The film ended with nothing in its plot resolved. The lights came up. The cinema emptied. I went, too, with everybody else, and as I did I saw that a sweater was still on the seat she'd been sitting in and a bag was still there tucked under it. But I went up the stairs to the proper exit. I walked straight past the ushers without telling them. They'd probably work it out for themselves when they found the bag and the sweater. They'd know to go down to the exit door and check.

But here I am now, awake in the middle of the night and asking myself whether she's still in there, on the other side of that door.

I know a story about that fire exit down there, you'd told me once in the cinema.

It was back before we knew each other very well, one of the first times we went to that cinema. The film we'd come to see had ended. The credits were rolling, huge above our heads. We stood up. You stretched and pointed and as you yawned I saw the clean wet insides of your mouth, and your tongue unfurling.

It's really illegal, you said through the yawn. It shouldn't be allowed. I don't know how they got away with it with the fire regulations people.

The cinema had been converted into a new cinema from an old cinema. Its downstairs was now a pub which claimed to sell the cheapest beer in Britain; there were often people throwing up outside this pub. Above it was the new cinema, three screens tucked into the skeleton of the upper half of the old cinema, which meant that the new cinema always smelt of fried food and sometimes the noise from the pub would shimmer through the soundtrack of whatever film you were watching. That night we had seen a film with Ralph Fiennes in it, something vaguely Russian. Eugene Onegin maybe. Was Liv Tyler in it? There were balalaikas on the soundtrack, or maybe I'm mixing that up with Dr Zhivago. I lie in bed now and try to remember. I can't really recall anything that happened in it, other than that there were love letters and a lot of fur and snow.

Come on, you'd said. I'll show you.

Nobody even noticed what we were doing. The doors were heavy, sheets of red painted metal. You leaned on the bar to open one side, then knelt down, took your newspaper out of your bag, chose one of its thinnest sections, folded it in two and shoved it under the near-closed door. This jammed it open just a crack – not quite open, not quite closed.

There beyond the fire door the plushness of the cinema simply stopped. The stairs were concrete. They smelt of disinfectant. The bulbs in the staircase ceiling were bare. We went down two flights of stairs and came to a door. It was locked.

It looked like it hadn't been used for a very long time. There was another door just along from it. It had no outside handle. I pushed against it. It wouldn't give.

You told me how you'd been given a tour of the cinema when it first opened by a friend of yours who was the manager of the cinema bar. This, he'd told you, was where he'd come with one of the young girl ushers, looking for three crates of bottled fruit juice which had been delivered via a back door, at least that's what he'd told *her*, as the fire exit door had swung closed on its own weight behind them and they went down the stairs and backed each other up against the walls. They'd had sex a few times. Then they'd found that mobile phone signals didn't work in there and they'd begun to panic. They'd run back upstairs and banged on the locked doors. They'd shouted, but they couldn't hear anything in there from the cinema, and even the noise from the noisiest pub in town wasn't coming through those thick bare brick walls.

They were there for a day and a half, you told me as we stood looking up at the bare steps, till a cleaning lady looking for somewhere for a sly smoke opened the fire door and found them both sitting there in separate corners with their arms round themselves, freezing cold on the concrete. It was winter, you explained.

That's when I had started to panic too, that the Arts and Books section you'd folded a couple of minutes ago wouldn't be substantial enough to hold the door against its own weight and that when we got back up the stairs it would have shut itself of its own accord, leaving us behind metal several inches thick with no way to open it, which is exactly when you'd pushed me back against the breeze-blocks and kissed me gently, then harder, on the mouth. I think of it now and something inside me acts like a film cliché, like my insides are a hollow guitar, and just the disembodied thought of the movement of your hands can do anything it likes, once, then again, then again, to the strings of it.

Hello? you say. What?

You sound a bit groggy.

It's me, I say.

It's half past three in the morning, you say.

I was just wondering how you are, I say.

You can't do this, you say. It isn't fair. It's unreasonable. We agreed not to behave like this. We promised.

I just need to ask you this thing, I say.

Christ, you say. I was asleep. I've got to get up in three hours.

I couldn't sleep, I say.

Bombs? Terrorists? London in flames? End of the world? Rough day at work? you say.

Well, you know that fire exit at the new cinema, I say.

The what? you say.

The fire exit that's not an exit, I say.

Not a what? you say.

What I was wondering, I say, is whether or not, if you were trapped in there, well, not you, I mean one, someone, anyone, if someone was trapped in there and the door had shut and everybody'd gone home, do you think there'd still be any lights on in there?

Eh, you say.

Do you think there's a general lighting panel in that cinema where all the lights, including the ones in the back corridors and stairs, get switched off last thing? I say. I mean, what if someone was trapped in there and nobody knew she or he was there? I mean, would he or she be standing waiting for someone to come and look for him or her, and then suddenly the lights would just flick off and that'd be it, dark in there till someone somewhere came in the next day and switched all the lights in the building on again?

Yes, but what kind of a fire exit has no way out? you say.

Or do you think the lights are always on in

there, I say, like emergency lighting, regardless of the cinema being open or closed?

It sounds illegal to me, you say. Where is this?

Don't you remember? I say.

The thing is, you don't. You don't remember anything about it, or about showing me it, or about you folding your magazine to keep the door open. You don't remember us calling it the fire excite on the way home. You don't remember anything.

Go back to bed, you say. Phone me in the morning. Phone me on my lunchbreak. Go to sleep now. It's the middle of the night. I'll call you tomorrow. Good night.

So I do as you say. I go back to bed. But then because you told me to do it and I did it, I get annoyed at myself and throw the duvet off me. It falls on to the floor.

I sit on the floor wrapped in the duvet in the dark.

I ask myself why I didn't go down and help the woman, or at least check that she didn't need help. I ask myself why I didn't just mention it to an usher on my way out. Why did I do that, why did I just walk out of the cinema like that, without a word, even though I knew someone might be having a rough time?

My phone buzzes in my hand. The screen says it's you.

Did I wake you? you say.

Yes, I lie. I was really deeply asleep. You did.

Sorry, you say.

Fair enough, I say. That makes us equal now.

I remembered something I wanted to tell you, you say.

About the cinema and the exit? I say.

No, about me walking home from town yesterday, you say.

You tell me how you were just walking along the road towards your new place and something hit you on the head, bounced off you and hit the road in front of you. You looked down at it on the pavement. It was a tiny McDonalds milk carton, rocking from side to side. A bus had just passed you. On its top deck was a bunch of adolescent girls. They were giving you the finger out of its back window. Then you watched them pass another pedestrian, a woman walking ahead of you. The girls threw a handful of the same small milk cartons out of the top window at her. Some of them hit her. She saw the girls in the bus giving her the finger. She stopped in the street. She bent down and picked up one of the tiny milk cartons and she threw it back at the bus.

This makes me laugh. You're laughing too; we're both laughing into each other's ears in different rooms, in different houses, in different parts of the city, at four a.m. in the morning.

It's getting light outside. The birds are waking up. I think about what it would be like to be in the dark and maybe not know what time it is. I tell you about the woman, how she went through the fire doors, and about her stuff left on the seat and under it.

There's no way out of there, I say. I'm amazed you don't remember. There was just a locked door, and another locked door next to it.

Well, there's nothing you can do about it now, you say. Someone will have found her, you say. They've probably sorted it now, you say. Regulations will have made them make it a proper exit by now, you say. She'll have walked through the wall like that man you once told me about, you say.

Like what man? I say.

The man who fell down between the wall and the soundproofing, you say. In the cinema, in your home town, when you were small. You told me that story. It was definitely you who told me. Remember?

No, I say.

Remember, you say. I'd had a really horrible day at work. I wanted to leave, but I couldn't, because of the loans. I felt terrible, remember?

I remember you feeling terrible a lot, I say.

Don't be horrible, you say. I was feeling really bad and you put me to bed and you curled up behind me very close, I was under the covers and you were on top of them, and you told me the story. You said your father had come home from work one day and told it at the dinner table and you'd never forgotten it. You said this man had come into the job centre and told him the story over the counter. And after you told me it I fell asleep, and in the morning I went to work and that was the day I handed in my notice.

I remember you handing in your notice, I say, but I don't remember any story about any, what was it, soundproofing?

I'll tell you again, you say. And then, with any luck, you'll go back to bed and you'll fall asleep. And so will I.

Yes, but I can't now, I say. Now that you've told me to it'll make me stay awake all the harder.

We both laugh again. It fills me with hope and sadness both at the same time.

And in the morning, you say, if you're still worried, you can call the cinema and ask them if anyone claimed the sweater and the bag, and if they say they've still got them in Lost Property you can tell them about the woman.

Then you tell me the following story. After you

do we hang up and I go back to bed. I rearrange the duvet round me. I put myself inside it. I tell myself as I fall asleep that when I wake up I'm going to call that cinema and threaten to report them if they haven't made that fire exit a real exit with a proper, easy, simple, push-bar-down way out.

A man is working in a cinema. It's the 1960s and all the local cinemas are under pressure to adapt to changes. It's widescreen or nothing. It's soundproofing and quadrophonic sound or bingo hall.

The man is helping to construct an internal wall parallel to the main wall of the building. The new wall is for soundproofing. It's made of plasterboard. Because the cinema is a large one, one with a balcony, the new wall is more than seventy feet high and the man is working at the very top of it, screwing it together. In a few more panels' time it will touch the ceiling.

He leans over the top ridge of it. The wall bends. He loses his footing on the scaffolding and he falls down between the two walls.

Because the walls are only a metre apart he hits and braces himself against one or the other as he falls, which lessens the momentum. He hits the ground with only a few scuffs and bruises and, he finds out later, a broken wrist. He's not sure whether he broke it in the fall or in the act of making his exit, because as he stands up and dusts himself down, miraculously almost unscathed, he realises he is trapped between the two walls.

He stands there, sandwiched between them in the dark, for less than a minute. Then he turns to the new wall and kicks it. It doesn't give. He kicks it again. He kicks and punches and throws himself against it until he makes a hole in the plasterboard. Then he rips his way out. He never knew he was so strong. His workmates, who've been running around in front of the internal wall like scared cats, clap him on the back.

But the firm that's converting the cinema sacks him for 'timewasting' and 'ruining cinema property'. He picks up his papers in his less sore hand and leaves the building. He goes to the doctor that afternoon, has himself signed off and has his wrist seen to.

Six weeks later he goes to the job centre to see what there might be for him in the way of similar work.

the second person

You're something else. You really are.

This is the kind of thing you'd do. Say you were standing outside a music shop. You'd go into that shop and just buy an accordion. You'd buy one that cost hundreds of pounds, one of the really big ones. It would be huge. It would be a pretty substantial thing just to lift or to carry across a room, never mind actually play.

You would buy this accordion precisely because you can't play the accordion.

You'd go into the shop. You'd go straight to the place they keep the accordions. You'd stand and look at them through the glass of the case. When the assistant, who'd have noticed you as soon as you came in – partly because you look (you always look) like a person of purpose and partly

because you happen to be, yes, very eye-catching –
came straight over to serve you, you'd point at the
one you wanted. The shop probably wouldn't have
that many makes of accordion, maybe just five or
six. You'd point at the one whose name you liked
the sound of best. You'd like the sound of a word
like Stephanelli more than you'd like the sound of
a word like Hohner. It would also be the one you
liked the look of best, with its frame (if that's
what they're called) made of light brown wood, a
good workaday colour; the other accordion makes
in the case would look too lacquered for you, too
varnished, less ready for the world.

When the assistant asked you if you'd like to try
the Stephanelli before you purchased it, you'd
simply hand her your bank card. You'd take the
heavy accordion home. You'd sit here on the
couch and heave it out of its box and on to your
knees. You'd press the button or unhook the
leather strap or whatever keeps its pleats shut.
You'd let it fall heavily open like a huge single
wing. You'd let it fill itself with air like a huge
single lung.

But then that thought of the accordion being a
bit like a single wing or a single lung would make
you uneasy. So this is what you'd do. You'd go back
to that shop. And although you can't really afford
it, although you can't even play one accordion,

never mind more than one, and although playing two accordions at once is actually humanly impossible, you would catch the eye of the same assistant and point into the glass case again, at the accordion next to the space left by the one you've just bought.

That one too, please, you'd say.

That's what you're like.

No it isn't, you say.

I feel you get annoyed beside me.

That's nothing like me, you say.

You move beside me on the couch. You move your arm, which has been tucked there between us against my side like a reassurance. You pretend you're doing this because you need to reach for your coffee cup.

I didn't mean it in a horrible way, I say. I meant it in a nice way.

But you're sitting forward now, not looking at me, looking away.

What amazes me about you, you say still looking away, is that after all these years, all the years of dialogue between us, you think you've got the right to just decide, like you're God, who I am and who I'm not and what I'm like and what I'm not and what I'd do and what I wouldn't. Well, you don't. Just because you've got, you know, a new life and a new love and a whole new day and dawn and dusk and everything new and shiny like in some glorious pop song, it doesn't make me a fiction you can play with or some well-known old used-up song you can choose not to listen to or choose to keep on repeat in your ears whenever you like just so you can feel better about yourself.

I don't need to feel better about myself, I say. And I'm not playing with anything. I'm not keeping anything on repeat.

But as I say it I notice there's something out of place on what was our window ledge. There's what looks like a piece of wood there I've never seen before. It's new, like the new mirror in the bathroom, the clothes in the kitchen by the washing machine that aren't really your style, the slight trace in the air of what was our house of the scent of something or someone else.

You don't put your arm back where it was. So I move too. I make it look like I'm moving to be more comfortable, to lean on the far arm of the couch. I look at the place on the couch arm where there's the old coffee cup ring. It's been there for years, we made it not long after we bought this couch. Hoovering it didn't remove it. Working at it with a brush and some kind of cleaning stuff only made the area of plush round it less plush, making it even more obvious. I can't remember which one of us is responsible for it, which one of us put the cup down that made that mark in the first place. I'm pretty sure it wasn't me, but I can't remember for definite. I trace the ring with my finger, then I trace the square of worn plush round it like a frame.

God, you're saying next to me now. *This is what you're like.*

You say it in a voice like it's supposed to be my voice, though in reality it's nothing like my voice.

This is what you're like, I say. I say it in the mimic voice you've just used.

You've really changed, you say.

No I haven't, I say.

You're so self-righteous now, you say. You're so unbelievable that if it was you who went into that music shop you just invented for me to be made to look wasteful and whimsical and stupid in –

I never said anything about stupid, I say. Or whimsical.

Yes, you did, you say. You suggested I'm wasteful and whimsical. You suggested, in your story of me buying musical instruments I can't play, that I'm completely ridiculous and laughable.

No I didn't, I say. I was actually trying to suggest –

Don't interrupt me, you say. You always –

No I don't, I say.

I know what you'd be like in that shop, you say. I know what it'd be like as soon as you pushed the door open.

What? I say. What then? What exactly? What would I be like?

I know exactly what you'd be like in there, you say.

Go on, I say. Go on, then. I'm longing to hear just exactly what you think of me.

You'd push open the door, you say –

I bet I know, I say. I bet I push open the door and I go really peremptorily to the counter and I ask to see every stringed instrument in the shop, and then I sit at the counter until the assistant brings the first one to me, it's a guitar, and she puts it down in front of me. And when she goes to get the next one I take a pair of pliers out of my bag. And I take the first string on the guitar and get a grip on it with the sharp bit of the pliers and then I cut it so it snaps. And then I cut the next string. And then I cut the next string. And the next, until I've done all the strings and I'm ready for the next guitar. Is that what happens? And then do I cut every string on every stringed thing in the shop? And do I take particular pleasure in cutting the many strings of the pretty harp that was in the window? Is that what happens? Is that what I'm like?

You are looking at me, shocked.

No, you say.

That's what you'd like to think, though, isn't it? I say. That's what you'd like to think about me.

You're looking at me now with your eyes guarded and hurt. What I was going to say was this, you say. Do you want to know what I was going to say?

No, I say.

You push open the door, you say, and it's like you've entered a Hollywood musical.

Oh, right. I see, I say.

There's a bright build of soundtrack, you say, and it starts when you push the door open and the bell above the door makes a little pinging sound. And you're in the place with all the pianos, and there's a man just sitting there playing the beginnings of a song like Taking a Chance on Love or Almost Like Being in Love or no, no, I know what it is, it's A Tisket, A Tasket, I Lost My Yellow Basket. And you can't help it, you lean forward over the piano to speak to the man and you say, did you know that this song was a huge hit for Ella Fitzgerald a mere year before Billie Holiday sang Strange Fruit? And if you put the two songs together and compare them you get a real picture of race politics and what was acceptable and what was true from that particular time in recent history? Think about it, you say to the man. They're both all about colour, but one's about what's really happening in the world, and the other's a piece of absurdist nonsense, like a denial that words could ever mean anything, about a girl who loses a yellow basket and doesn't know where she'll find it. And guess which one was the huge hit-parade hit and stayed at number one for seventeen weeks?

So I'm a know-all, I say. Right. I see.

And the man smiles at you and keeps playing, you say, and then someone else on another piano joins in behind him in a harmony, and then another person on one of the others, until the whole room is a mess of joyful piano harmony, and you go on into the next room where the violins and so on are for sale, you can still hear the pianos in the background, and then three rather beautiful girls on fiddles pick up the tune too, and it's romantic, the song has turned into a very romantic version of itself. And you tell the girls as you go past, did you know that there's actually a much less famous follow-up song where Ella Fitzgerald finds her yellow basket again after all? It's almost better than the original, well, I prefer it, though it wasn't such a huge hit at the time. And the pretty violinists nod and smile, and as if to oblige you all round you the tune

everybody's suddenly playing is the follow-up
tune, the tune you just mentioned, and now the
whole shop is resounding with it, the horn
department full of people playing trumpets and
saxes and clarinets which flash in the lights from
the shop ceiling and the noise they make,
complementing the pianos and the strings, is as
wide as a sky. The trumpet player at the front
winks at you and there's a girl on the sax who
winks too. Then you go into the next room and
the next room is full of children on kazoos,
ocarinas, recorders, glockenspiels, chime bars,
castanets, they're all joining in, playing the same
tune, in fact anywhere, everywhere you go, up or
down the stairs, from department to department
people are playing the same happy tune on every
single instrument in this shop, it's like the whole
shop is alive, its walls are moving to the rhythm,
and the tune builds and builds, only threatening
to come to an end, only fading down, as you
walk towards the shop door and reach your hand
out to open it. Down, down, down goes the tune,
but then, just to see what will happen, you let
the door handle go and you take three steps back
from the door, and like a joke the music soars out
really loud again. And then, on the right rhythm,
the perfect final three notes, you open the door,
go through the door, shut the door, and the whole

thing ends on the single ping of the bell as you close it behind you.

There, you say. That's what you're like.

I am on my feet now. I am furious.

So, I say. So I'm a naïve know-all boring unbearable self-dramatist who goes around the world thinking I'm really special, really something, really it? And wherever I go I take it for granted that everything in the whole world is nothing but a cutesy orchestra there to perform for me? Just to please me? As if the whole world can be controlled? As if the whole world's there just to play my own private soundtrack?

You know I didn't mean it like that, you say.

You look cowed. I feel suddenly very righteous.

And you think I'm the kind of person who'd maunder on, in a situation where it was totally inappropriate, about how one song is really more important than another song because of politics, yet really, in reality, I'd prefer to wallow about in some kitschy old nonsense that feeds my delusions of grandeur?

Eh? you say.

You look astonished.

That's how supercilious? That's how solipsistic? I say.

I never said anything about solipsistic, you say. I

don't even know what it means. I never said super anything. You're misunderstanding me.

You think I'm pedantic and irresponsible! I yell. Don't you?

You're on your feet too now. You're shouting too. You shout something about a basket case. You shout that you're not shallow or knowledgeless or wasteful or the kind of person who'd buy an accordion because of its brand name. Then, in a list of smarting adjectives, you tell me what I am.

What I am is out through the front door.

What I do is close it behind me with a self-righteous slam.

All the way across town, alongside the still-resonating slam of the door behind me, I have that maddening song in my head about the girl who loses her yellow basket. When I get back to the flat there's nobody else in and I sit on the step between the kitchen and the living room and try to think up adjectives for you, adjectives I could fling at you like sharp little stones, but all I can really hear in my head is the argument Ella Fitzgerald is having with the boys in her band:

> Was it green?
> No no no no!
> Was it red?

No no no no!
Was it blue?
No no no no!

I think I remember Ella Fitzgerald's voice becoming more and more comically annoyed at the backing singers getting the colour wrong each time, so that by the time she sings the final string of no's she sounds almost irate.

Then I start to wonder if I've remembered the order of the colours in the argument correctly.

I go over to the pile of CDs. They're my CDs; they weren't hard to take with me, you're not really one for jazz. I find the right one. I look on the listings for A Tisket, A Tasket. I insert it into the machine and keep the button pressed in until it reaches track eight.

The song is a piece of blunt charm, the way it courts misery then glances away from it with a loss at the heart of it that's not really a loss after all, or a loss that's pretending not to be a loss, and the slight hoarseness of Ella Fitzgerald's younger, gruffer self as she sings it is so blithe, almost as if unaware of the modulation her voice will soon be capable of when she's older and she's wiser. But what is it all about, in the end? What's the mysterious basket? Who's the mysterious little girl who steals it? Why will Ella Fitzgerald die if she doesn't get it back? When it ends I am sitting on the step laughing at you calling me a basket case; I am laughing so much with my arms round myself and at the same time am so near tears that the next track on the CD, the song's near-twin, I Found My Yellow Basket, takes me by surprise.

The boys in the band who sing with Ella Fitzgerald on this second song are very gracious. They offer to cover the cost, for her, of the loss of her original basket in the other song. Oh no, you don't have to, she tells them, I've got good news for you, and I realise, hearing the lightness in her voice as she sings about how now she's on her way, feeling light and gay, what a total relief it is that there's a song in the world where Ella Fitzgerald gets to track down that mysterious hidden basket-stealing girl and find the missing yellow basket. She sings about how happy she is. Then she sings the word *now* for the last time. It sounds so innocent, so like the happy peal of a bell, that I feel ashamed.

The doorbell goes.

Outside the door is a large black box. It looks expensive. It looks new. It's so big it comes up to nearly my waist. The man who's brought it up all the stairs is red and breathless. I sign for it and drag it inside. It's very heavy. At first I have no idea what can be in it.

Then it dawns on me what's in there, of course it is, with its black and white keys in the dark.

I know neither of us will have the first idea how to play one, never mind even open and close one properly. It'll take some learning. I open the note that came with it instead. I presume, as I do, that it'll tell me that this is one of a pair and that if I'm looking for the other one it's over at yours.

This is what the note says:

You're something else, you. You really are.

i know something you don't know

The boy had come home from school one lunchtime in May and gone to his bed. He'd been every day in his bed now for nearly four months, all the bad summer. In those early weeks he had still made the effort to sit up in the morning when she went in to open the curtains. For the past couple of weeks all he'd done was open his eyes, not even moving his head on the pillow.

It was a condition which didn't show up on tests. It was most likely a post-viral condition. Three different doctors had seen him: the GP, a consultant paediatrician at the hospital and, last month, a different, private, top consultant paediatrician who held clinics in one of the big houses in the rich part of the city, did all the same tests on the boy's feet and hands, looked into his eyes and ears, took blood. The results had been inconclusive and had cost £800. Now it was August. When she had gone into his room to open the curtains this morning he'd kept his eyes shut and in a small voice from the bed had said: please don't.

The boy's mother went into the kitchen and got out the Yellow Pages.

Under Healers it said See Complementary Therapies.

Complementary Therapies was between Compensation Claims and Composts, Peats and Mulches. Only two of the therapists listed were local. One was called Heavenly Health Analysis Ltd. Complimentary health care treatment, holistic health screening. Inner journey Indian head massage. Stress, worries. Hopi candle ear wax removal. Herbal advice line, health problems, etc. Outstanding accurate understanding from qualified registered therapist Karen Pretty.

The other advertising box had only three words in it and a number.

Nicole. Trust me. 260223.

The boy's mother dialled the first number. It was a machine. There was stringy music. A calm voice over the top of the music said Hello caller. You are welcome. Leave your details, including the important information of how you found this contact number for Heavenly Health Analysis Limited, after the tone.

Hello, she said. I found your number in the Yellow Pages. I would be very much obliged if you could ring me back regarding a serious health matter.

She dialled the second number. She let the phone ring in case an answerphone had to be activated. It rang thirty times. When she took it away from her ear and held it up in front of her to press the end of calls button, a tiny distant word shot out of the plastic in her hand.

What?

Eh, hello? the boy's mother said.

Yes, what? the voice said in her ear.

I'm trying to get in touch with a person called Nicole, the boy's mother said. I found the number in –

Come on, for Christ's sake, what? the voice said.

It's my son, she said.

I charge £50 a visit, the voice said.

Yes, the boy's mother said.

Where do you live? the voice said. Hurry up. I really need to go to the toilet.

The boy's mother told the voice the address and where to turn right at the roundabout if coming by car but the voice had hung up or been cut off, she couldn't tell when, somewhere in the list of directions, and she was left saying hello? into the phone, to nobody.

Before she'd had to stay at home all day because of the boy, she had been an assistant clerk in the office of a company which made a lot of money installing digital phone networks all over the Third World. The Third World was still open territory for phones. The company also set up cheap mobile deals with Eastern European countries, using secondhand mobiles people traded in for updated phones here in the West. Voices all over Eastern Europe were talking right now on old UK phones; this was something she'd liked thinking about, before. It was a funny and interesting thought that someone with a different life and a totally incomprehensible (to her) language might be talking to someone, arguing with someone, whispering secrets or sorting everyday things about shopping or family down what might be her old phone.

But it wasn't amusing to think any more, not in the same way, now that what she talked about down the phone to her mother or to the people from work were things she didn't really want to hear come out of her mouth, about what the boy wasn't doing, like eating much today. Or wanting to watch TV, even the cartoons. Or letting himself be got up without a fuss so he could be carried through to go to the bathroom. Or even responding at all any more when she sat on his bed and asked him questions: do you want to watch the cartoons? Will I put the football DVD in? Is it sore in your eyes? Where in your head? Too bright? Too dark? Do you want the light on? Off?

The phone in her hand rang. Caller unknown. She watched it ring. She let it click into answerphone then waited for it to tell her that it had received a new voicemail message. She played the message back. It was the voice of Karen Pretty from Heavenly. It offered three initial consultation times. The boy's mother phoned straight back and left her choice on Heavenly's answerphone.

The doorbell rang. It was after lunch, after the boy had shrunk back into the sheets away from the plate saying he was too cold, and after she'd sat at the dining-room table downstairs and eaten, herself, the two fish fingers and the microwave chips she'd put on the plate for him.

There was a rough-looking woman at the door. She was middle-aged and sloppily dressed in a stained long t-shirt and black leggings.

Fifty up front cash, the woman said. Where's the, what's it again, a boy? Is he in his bed?

She had her foot in the door. The boy's mother explained, holding the door, that she'd engaged someone else.

Yeah, right, the woman said. Karen Pretty, ear wax queen. Can't even spell complementary medicine right and you're letting her near something you love. I wouldn't. Each to their own. Karen Pretty. KP nuts is what I call her.

The woman had got into the house. She was standing in the hall now, looking past the boy's mother up the stairs.

I'll take a cheque if it's made out to cash, she said on her way up.

Her bulk made the stairwell look small. She held out her hand to keep the boy's mother at the foot of the stairs. She breathed like a heavy smoker; her breath was audible over the traffic noise through the open door.

Be down in a minute, she said. Hurry with that cheque, will you?

It was true; it was only about a minute, maybe even less, before she was wheezing down again and standing in the doorway of the sitting room.

I've no idea what's wrong with him, she said. He'll probably be okay. By the way, can I get a glass of water?

The boy's mother went to the kitchen and filled a beer glass with tap water. When she came back the front door was shut, the cheque had gone from the arm of the armchair with the chequebook and the bank card, there was no sign of the woman anywhere up or down the street outside the house and it wasn't till half an hour later when she looked for her handbag that she realised it was gone as well and so were the two Capo Di Monte figurines, gone from the sideboard.

Seated Lady And Child. Clown Balancing A Ball.

Karen Pretty from Heavenly Health Analysis Ltd came at the appointed time two days later even though the boy's mother had cancelled her by answerphone. She was on crutches. She stood precariously on the rug in the middle of the sitting room.

Do you have a hard upright chair? she said. Like a dining-room chair? Thank you very much. I'd just like to make it clear that I don't intend to charge you for this visit because it is an initial consultation visit. Can you put the chair exactly here?

She drew a line on the floor with the end of a crutch.

Bless you, she said.

She was too young to say bless you. She looked about twenty-five. She had long brown hair held back with a clasp at the nape of her neck. She looked familiar to the boy's mother.

Do you not work at the Abbey National? she asked the girl.

Karen Pretty put her crutches neatly together, held them in the one hand and sat down in the middle of the room.

You probably know by now that Nicole Campbell of Trust Me is in the process of being prosecuted by the CPS for fraud, she said. I feel for you, Mrs Haig, what's your first name, please?

Harriet, the boy's mother said.

I can feel you are carrying pain, Harriet, Karen Pretty said. I feel that someone full of sadness lives in this house.

Karen Pretty, eyes closed, smiled and nodded.

White, she said or maybe, Quite.

Are you going to be able to get upstairs? the boy's mother said. Only, that's where he is.

Where who is? Karen Pretty said still with her eyes shut.

My son. Anthony. He's the one who's ill, the boy's mother said.

Yes. Somehow I sensed, Karen Pretty said, that I would be doing a tarot reading for a boy who couldn't get down some stairs today.

She opened her eyes, looked into her shoulder bag, took something out and held it up.

I could carry him down, the boy's mother said.

Oh no, we don't actually need him actually bodily in the room with us, Karen Pretty said.

She unwrapped a little wooden box from inside a piece of red silk.

I charge fifty pounds per reading, she said. But I intend not to charge you, Harriet, for today's session. The guides have asked me not to.

The Girl Guides? the boy's mother thought. She imagined them all in the uniforms of her own childhood, standing in a blue line all shaking their heads at Karen Pretty.

They say you will remember this kindness and repay my kindness amply in the future with your own kindness, Karen Pretty said.

No, if you don't mind I'd much prefer to –, the boy's mother said.

He is carrying pain, Karen Pretty suddenly said. His spirit is very strong. Is he a headstrong kind of a boy?

Well, no, the boy's mother said.

Yes, that's right, Karen Pretty said.

Karen Pretty and the boy's mother sat in silence for half a minute or so. It felt like a very long time. It was long enough to feel embarrassing. Then Karen Pretty put her hand out and presented a worn pack of cards to the boy's mother.

Your mother is going to shuffle them for you, Anthony, she said to the fireplace.

The boy's mother blushed. She shuffled the cards and handed them back to Karen Pretty who turned one up, then the next, then the next, and laid them beside each other on her knees.

A struggle for position will end in improvement, she said pointing at the boy on top of a hill with a stick, fighting off a lot of people below him with sticks. A difficult journey to a calmer place, she said pointing at the boat full of swords in the water. A reawakening, she said pointing to the family climbing out of a grave beneath a giant set of wings. I am not going to charge you the usual £50 for this reading, she said gathering the cards and putting the pack together again.

The boy's mother insisted. She gave Karen Pretty two folded twenties and a ten. Karen Pretty took the money and put it down on the carpet by the chair leg. She called a taxi firm on her mobile. The two women sat in silence while they waited. Karen Pretty smiled a sweet smile at the boy's mother and shrugged her eyebrows high into her forehead. She sighed. She hummed a tune. She was patient as if patience was a part of her remit.

Peace to you, Harriet, she said when the taxi drew up outside the house.

She leaned on her crutches to get to her feet. The boy's mother watched her back herself on to the seat of the taxi and watched the taxi drive away. She looked round the room, in which there was more than a trace of Karen Pretty's perfume. She opened the window. She put the dining-room chair back in the dining room. She went to the kitchen and came back with a wet cloth. She wiped the chair down. Then, in the sitting room, she kicked the folded money across the carpet till it disappeared under the sofa.

She went upstairs to check. He was asleep. His short out-breaths made her own breathing hurt.

That night, though she'd already undressed and got into bed, she made herself get up again and come downstairs. In the kitchen over the sink she struck a safety match and set the two twenty-pound notes and the ten alight together and held them so they burned all the way to her hand. She flushed the black stuff they left down the sink then wiped the sink clean and dry with the tea-towel. She went back to bed. She realised she had forgotten to check on him like she always did when she got to the top of the stairs. She got up again. She stood at the crack in the door and saw his head on the pillow in the dark.

She lay in bed with the light off and her eyes

wide open because this time, she knew, she'd been robbed.

The boy was in bed. It had been days and days. It was September. His mother had come in to do the curtains for the morning and he had let her open them.

He could see from here a whiteness which was really the side of one of the houses opposite. But it looked like snow. It was snow. It was a wide square of snow the size of a house, snow even though it was summer.

He watched to see if it would melt, because the morning sun was sending a squinted rectangle of yellow through the gaps in the houses on his own side of the street on to the white. But the snow was super-snow, mega-strength multi-snow. No sun could melt it. If you picked it up to mould it into a snowball would it be cold on your hands or warm? A warm snowball. It would be impossible.

The boy was tired. All this thinking of snow was making him tired. But now he was thinking of how you would make a snowball out of warm snow and your bare hands would stay their usual colour and not get cold or red in the process.

The bear was at the bottom of the bed. It was the big bear, the one his father had brought back three years ago, when he'd been abroad for work, away for a long time for the first time. The bear had come from an airport. It was huge. It was nearly the same size as the boy.

He reached out in front of him until it was like his hand was touching the white square he could see through the window. It was snow. He took some of the snow in his hand. Because it was warmed snow it didn't feel unpleasant to touch. He took his other hand out from under the covers and used both hands to mould the snowball. Then he aimed it at the bear at the bottom of the bed and threw it.

The boy's arm hurt a little from the throw.

He put it back under the covers.

Next thing he'd do was: he would shift out of the bed when the bear least expected it and sneak up without it noticing and punch the bear right in the mouth. Then he would wrestle it. Though it would fight back hard, he'd beat it. He'd kick it. He'd bite it in the ear. He'd eat the bear. He'd totally beat it completely till it roared that it gave in.

Yesterday if he'd thought he'd wrestle a bear or make a snowball or something like that it would have made his head go the sore empty way, not like snow was a white place on an opposite wall, not like summer snow, but like there was only snow, nothing else, nothing but being in it, everything a sort of snow.

Today he shifted a little out of the covers. He did it quietly so the bear wouldn't suspect.

He began to feel a little hungry.

He slid a little further out, then a little, careful, more.

writ

I sit my fourteen-year-old self down opposite me at the table in the lounge so that we can have a conversation, because all she's done so far, the whole time she's been here in my house, is ignore me, stare balefully at a spot just above my head, or look me in the eye then look away from me as if I'm the most boring person on the planet.

I come home from work today and she's here again. I don't ask why, or where she's been since she was last here. I ask her instead to turn down the television. I ask her again to come and sit down at the table.

She sighs. She finally does as I ask. She pulls out a chair clumsily. It is almost as if she is being clumsy on purpose. She sits down, sighs audibly again.

Last week someone, a girl, a woman I hardly know (now when does a girl become a woman? when exactly do we stop being girls?) turned towards me as we walked along a busy street, backed me expertly up against the wall of a builder's restoration of a row of old shops in the middle of London in broad daylight, and kissed me. The kiss, out of nowhere, took me by surprise. When I got home that night my fourteen-year-old self was roaming about in my house knocking into things, wild-eyed and unpredictable as a blunt-nosed foal in a house would be.

It is shocking to see yourself like you haven't been for nearly thirty years. It is also a bit embarrassing, having yourself around, watching your every move as if watching your every move is the last thing that could possibly interest anyone.

What do you reckon to the house, then? I say. Do you like it?

She barely glances round her. She shrugs.

Would you like some coffee? I ask.

She does it again, the insolent look-then-look-away. She makes insolence a thing of beauty. For a moment how good she is at it actually makes me proud and I nod.

You go, girl, I say.

She looks at me as if I'm insane.

Where? she says.

Ha, I say. No, *you go, girl* is a phrase, like a cliché. It's from music. It means good on you, too right, that kind of thing. It's American. It's borrowed from black culture. It's from later. I mean, you're too young for it.

She makes a tch noise, almost non-existent.

I put the mug of coffee down on the table for her. She picks it up.

Use the coaster, I say.

She is looking at what's in the mug in horror.

No, because I need it to have milk in it, she says and her accent is so where I'm from and so unadulterated that hearing her say more than four words in a row makes my chest hurt inside.

I've no milk, I say. I forgot you took it with milk.

Also it's, like, the too-strong kind, she says. It's a bit too strong for me.

She says it quite apologetically.

It's all I've got in, I say.

I like the instant kinds of it, she says. The other kinds taste too much.

Yes, but instants are full of freezing agents, I say. They do all sorts of damage to your synapses –

By the time I've got to the word freezing and agents in this sentence her eyes have gone blank again. She pushes the cup away and puts her head in her hands. I feel suddenly forlorn. I want to say: look, aren't you amazed I ever even managed to buy a house? Don't you like how full of books it is? You like books. You don't have to pretend you're not clever to me. I know you are. I'd have loved the idea of a house full of books like this when I was your age.

Was I really going to say that: when I was your age? Would I really have found myself saying that appalling phrase out loud?

There are quite a few things, though, that I do want to say to her. Concerning our mother for instance, I want to say something like: don't worry, she'll be okay. It's a bad time now, that's all. She doesn't die until you're more than twice the age you are now.

But I can't say that, can I?

I want to say: your exams come out fine all the way down the line. You'll do all right at university. You'll have a really good time. Don't worry that you don't get off with that boy who smells of the linoleum at Crombie Halls of Residence in the first week. You don't have to get off with someone in Freshers' Week, it's not necessary, it's not important.

I want to tell her who to trust and who not to trust; who her real good friends are and who's going to fuck her over; who to sleep with, and who definitely not to. Definitely say yes to this person, it's one of the best things that's going to happen to you. And don't be alarmed, I want to say, when you find yourself liking girls as well as boys. It's okay. It's good. It works out very well. Don't even bother yourself worrying about it, not for a single afternoon, not for a single hour in a single afternoon. Don't, by the way, vote Labour in 1997; it's like a vote for the Tories. No, really. And when you're twenty-two and you go for the sales job in the middle of Edinburgh and you're backing the Citroen down the road where the Greyfriars Bobby statue is, don't back it so far, just go careful on the clutch, don't panic, because what happens when you panic is you totally collapse the back mudguard against the wall of the pub there and anyway there's no point in you even going for a job like that, I mean you get into the room and they're all wearing their power suits and you're wearing your jeans, so just, you know, know yourself a bit better, that's all I'm saying.

But I look at her sitting there, thin and insolent and complete, and I can't say any of it. It'd be terrible to proffer a friend she hasn't met yet who then turns out not to be a friend, or a left wing government that turns out not to be. Terrible to tell her, now, about a crushed mudguard one afternoon in 1984. It's somehow terrible even to suggest she'll go to university.

You need to eat more, I say instead.

She puts the end of her hair in her mouth. She takes it out and holds it up and fans it out, examines the wet hair for split ends.

Aw, don't do that, I say, it's disgusting.

She rolls her eyes.

She is spotty round the mouth and in the crevices down the side of her nose, of course she is, with a skin that I now know to call combination dry and greasy. I could tell her how to deal with it. Her middle parting makes her hair look flat and makes her look more cowed than she is. There's a constellation of acne on her forehead beneath it. I could tell her how to deal with that too.

I go and stand at the window and look out. That kiss up against the building site fills the inside of my head again as if someone had opened a lid at the top of my skull, poured in a jug of warm water mixed with flower food, then arranged a bunch of spring flowers in me – cheerfulness, daffodils – using me as the vase. But the light is coming down, February, early dusk, and the common is still patchy with snow. I know, now, though I didn't know it when I bought this house, that the common is actually a common burial ground; it's where they buried most of this city's thousands of plague-dead centuries ago.

Beneath the feet of the dogwalkers and the people coming back from the supermarket, under the grass and the going snow, under the mound where the paths all come together, are all the final shapes their lives took, all the bare bones. Above them the black of the common, and above it the sky the deep blue it goes just before dark. It's a clear night. The stars'll be out later. It'll be beautiful, all the stars and planets spread in their winter-spring alignments above the common. Are the stars out tonight? I don't know if it's cloudy or bright. Cause I only have eyes. Art Garfunkel, it was. The song coming into my head gives me an idea.

What's number one right now? I say. In the top twenty?

Figaro by the Brotherhood of Man, she says. It's appalling.

They're appalling, I say.

It's music for, like, infants, she says.

And that song Angelo, I say.

I hate that song, she says. It's crap.

It's such a steal from the Abba song Fernando, I say. You just have to think about it and it's so obvious.

Yeah, she says. It is. It's like really a steal. They just took the idea Abba had and they wrote it into a so much less good song.

Her voice, for the first time since she's been here, sounds almost enthusiastic. I don't turn round. I rack my brains to remember something she'll like.

I sing: Hey you with the pretty face. Welcome to the human race.

I really really like the way the piano they use in Mr Blue Sky has an electronic voice and you think it might even be the voice the sky has, if the sky had a voice, she says. I actually really really like that whole idea of an electric light orchestra because of the idea of, like, light-orchestral kind of thing, and then on top of that the idea that it's electric and that it's nothing but an electric light, like one you switch on and off.

It is the most she's said so far, the whole time she's been in the house.

Like a whole orchestra at the flick of a switch, I say.

A whole huge orchestra inside one lightbulb, she says. It's really clever to do that like with just writing some words together, it's really good the words doing all that by themselves. I really like it. Do you know that thing about the phrase written water?

No, I say.

That thing about the historic poet John Keats Miss Aberdeen in English told us today, she says.

The tragic pop star of the Romantic period, I say. Did Miss Aberdeen not say that?

Yeah, but when he died, my fourteen-year-old self says, like, before he died, the poet John Keats, right, apparently he said to someone, put it on my gravestone that here lies a poet whose name is written water. Not written down, but written water. Water that was written on. I think that's really beautiful. Here lies a poet whose name was written water.

One, I say. Not a poet. It says on the stone, here lies one.

Well, same thing, she says.

And it's writ in water, I say. It's three words, not two.

No, it's written, like one word, she says.

It isn't, I say. It's writ. Then in. Then water.

Yeah, but writ isn't a word, she says.

It is a word, actually, I say.

Yeah, like half a word, my fourteen-year-old self says. It doesn't mean anything.

It's a real whole word by itself, I say. You can find it in any dictionary. It's changed its meaning over time and at the same time it's kept its meaning. We just don't use the word exactly like that, in that form, any more these days.

I can hear her kicking at the bar under the table.

Don't do that, I say.

She stops it. She goes silent again. I look out over the darkening grass. I don't have to look round to know what she's doing, still swinging her leg under the table behind me but just above the bar, just expertly missing it every time.

He did die unbelievably young, you know, Keats, I say.

No he didn't, she says. He was twenty-five or something.

A joy forever, I say. Its loveliness increases. I can't remember what comes after nothingness. God. I used to know that poem off by heart.

We did a poem by him, she says.

Which one? I say.

The one about looking in an old book, she says. And oh yeah, I forgot. Because when I got into school this morning, it was really appalling because the art teacher made me take off my clothes. In front of everyone.

I turn round.

He what? I say.

Not he, she says. Miss MacKintosh. Weirdo.

Don't call Miss MacKintosh that, I say. Miss MacKintosh is really nice.

She's a weirdo from weirdoland, she says.

No she isn't, I say.

Like, she said to me you've to take off the

soaking wet things and put them on the radiator and you can wear my coat. I had to sit in her coat the whole way through double period art. My hands were freezing. I had to put them in the pockets a couple of times. My tights were ripped though, from the stones on the way down on the Landscaping. Then Laura Wise from 3B said she wasn't cold and gave me hers. She saw it happen. She said John McLintock was spazzodelic.

Wait a minute, I say. First, I don't think you should use that word. And second. What stones? Soaking wet, why exactly?

That boy John McLintock pushed me down the Landscaping, she says.

I remember the Landscaping; we used to hang around the Landscaping a lot. I don't remember anything about this, though. We used to pass the Landscaping every day on the way to school then home again. It was the green slope at the back of the houses where they kept what was left of the original wasteground they built the two estates on. Presumably there was some planning prohibition and that was why they couldn't cover the whole thing with houses; instead they pulled up the trees and grassed over the stubby bushes all the way to the new car park. The Landscaping was quite steep, if I remember rightly.

A boy was pushing people off it? I say.

Just me, she says. He only pushed me off it.
Nobody else. There were loads of us.

And you were on top of the Landscaping
because? I say.

Because of the new snow, she says.

Let me get this right, I say. He pushed –

It was slippy, she says.

She covers her face. She's smiling under her
hands, still sitting at the table with the cold coffee
in front of her, swinging her leg underneath the
table just above the bar of it. I realise I don't know
whether she's smiling because a boy pushed her
down a hill, because a girl picked her up at the
bottom of it or because an art teacher I know she's
got a crush on asked her to take off her clothes.

Then I realise it's because of all three. I
remember my hands in the warm pockets of the
adult coat.

It moves me. She can see this on my face and
she gets annoyed again. Her smile disappears. She
scowls.

Written is so much better than writ, she says.

It might be better but it isn't what it actually
says on the gravestone, I say.

Weirdo, she says.

Don't be rude, I say.

From weirdoland, she says almost under her
breath.

She gives me the quick look and then, with perfect timing, the artful look away.

Completely night now out beyond my house and only six o'clock in the evening. All the streetlights are on. All the cars in the city beyond are nosing their ways home or their ways away from home, making the noise traffic makes in the distance. Closer to home, out on the unlit common, under a sky that promises frost, someone invisible to us is rattling across one of the nearby paths on a bike, shouting and shouting. I love you, he shouts, or she shouts, hard to tell which, and then calls out what sounds like a name in the dark, shouted into the starry air above all the thousands of old dead, and then the words I love you again, and then again the name.

My fourteen-year-old self looks towards the window and so do I.

You hear that? we both say at once.

astute fiery luxurious

A parcel arrived. It looked really creepy. There was nobody in the house but me. I phoned you. You were still at work and very busy.

Uh huh, what now? you said.

A weird parcel came, I said. It's got our house number on it and the correct postcode and everything, but it's not addressed to us and I didn't notice until after the postie had gone.

I told you the name on the parcel. You said you'd never heard of him or her.

Me neither, I said.

It's just a misdelivery, you said. We'll put it back in the post tomorrow. Look, I'm busy. I've got to go. Are the pills working? Are you still sore?

A bit, I said.

Have a sleep on the couch, you said.

I can't, I said. I am less than one person in a hundred and the pills are keeping me awake.

Go and watch daytime TV, then, you said. It's your prerogative. You're signed off.

I can't, I said. I am less than one person in a hundred and the pills are making me sleepy. Plus I am now unable to operate machinery.

I'll bring supper, you said laughing. Listen, I've got to go.

You hung up. The laughing had made me feel a bit better. But when I went back into the front room the parcel was still there.

Last week we were in the supermarket and saw they were selling Swingball. I hadn't played it for twenty years and got nostalgic about how good I used to be at it. We bought it, stuck its metal stick in the lawn and played it. The next day I kept hearing a crackling noise, first when I was on my bike, then whenever I went up or down stairs. The noise was coming from under the skin of my left knee. Then the knee got sore, then the leg. Then I woke in the middle of the night unable to move anything from the shoulders down without it hurting. For the past three days I had been taking anti-inflammatories and lying on the couch monitoring myself for any of the fifty-nine side effects the leaflet warned were to varying degrees possible (including stomach pain, dizziness, changes in blood pressure, swollen legs, feet, face, lips, tongue or all of these, indigestion, heartburn, nausea, diarrhoea, headache, itchy skin, abdominal bloating, constipation, chest pain, vomiting, ringing in ears, weight gain, vertigo, depression, blurred vision, hair loss, serious kidney problems, inability to sleep, sleepiness, paranoia, hallucinatory episodes, and heart failure). So far I had possibly had two or three of them. But I wasn't sure if my ankles and feet had always been that shape, or whether I was imagining the high airy humming in my ears, like a faraway sea. Was I depressed? I had been getting up off the couch every few hours and checking myself in the mirror for weight gain.

Then the parcel had come. I had limped to the door and taken it from the postman without hesitation. But as soon as I had taken it I had known there was something wrong with it. It looked like it should have been heavier than it was, but when I had it in my hands it felt unnaturally light. It felt unnatural. There it still was. I wasn't wrong. It was odd. The writing on it was a crazy person's writing, scrawled all over the place. It was funny to see the address of our house in that unstable writing. The brown paper of it was old and soft, sellotaped very stiffly all over, as if it were a kind of shell rather than a parcel. It looked as if it had been going around the postal system for years. But it was postmarked yesterday. I couldn't make out where from.

I blinked. I was being paranoid. It was a side effect. It looked nothing more than, nothing worse than, an old-fashioned sci-fi TV programme prop, some pretend-evil creature with a name like molluscopod jerkily sliming across a makeshift landscape to evil synthesizer music chasing the sidekick girl.

I tried to think this, but the parcel defied me. It had been sent. It had been meant for someone.

I picked it up and carried it through to the kitchen and put it on the table, then I had a terrible urge to wash my hands. After this I went back through to the couch and switched on the TV. I watched the quiz where people are given random consonants and vowels and have to make up words. Then I watched another where people are eliminated if they give enough wrong answers. In the ad break I went back through to the kitchen. I had to. It was there on the table, too close to things in the fruit bowl that we would eventually eat.

I broke a banana off the bunch and poked the parcel over a few inches, away from the bowl, right to the edge of the table. I went to put the banana in the bin, holding the end which had touched the parcel well away from me. This was when you arrived home.

Why are you throwing away a perfectly good banana? you asked.

Then you looked at the parcel.

You looked at the writing on the parcel, the name and address. You picked it up and shook it. You shook your head. You looked at me. I shook my head too. You put it back down on the table and we both stepped back. We stared at it for a while. Then you said: it's something horrible, isn't it?

I nodded.

What if we just opened it? you said.

Well, it's something horrible. And it's not addressed to us, I said.

All through supper it got harder to breathe. I could hardly swallow. I felt dizzier and dizzier. You looked pale, appalled. You sat on the carpet, leaned against the armchair. You didn't eat; you flicked little bits of jalapeno off your pizza back into the pizza box.

What if, you eventually said, it had arrived here actually open? Split, you know, by accident.

Just split enough so we could see what was actually in it? I said.

Uh huh, you said.

I took the kitchen knife through and washed the pizza off it and dried it. You came through to the kitchen. You turned the parcel round on the table and took the knife. You cut right into it.

Christ, you said.

The smell was awful. We both stepped back. Then you took a deep breath, held your breath, unlocked the back door and took the sagging parcel and the knife outside. I heard you cough and I heard the ripping noise the knife made in the side of it. You coughed and then spat. I went out into the garden.

On the path beside the gaping parcel was a pile of filthy rags. The smell was foul.

Look, you said. I think it's pyjamas.

There was a jacket and a pair of small trousers for a six or seven year old. They were dark blue under the filth, and patterned with soiled and ruined little pictures, a child dressed as a guardsman, a child on a hobby horse, a child in a sports car, a child making a sandcastle.

There was a note. It said, in the same wild ballpoint writing: W H o S A n A U G H t Y B o Y t H E n.

Well, it's definitely not to either of us then, you said.

Jesus, I said.

Very weird, you said.

Beats me, I said.

Someone's mother? you said. Or father?

Someone's lover? I said.

Someone very angry, you said. Or unhappy.

Or a bad joke, I said.

A very bad joke. Or something much worse than a joke, you said.

Over our heads birds sang the evening down. You used the knife to prod the note and the clothes back through the parcel's mouth. I went to fetch the sellotape.

We came back inside. We locked the door. You washed your hands under the tap. I went to the bathroom to wash mine. I ran the water until it was very hot. Even after using the soap someone brought us from France, the one with the too-strong smell, I couldn't get the other smell out of my nose.

It was half past two in the morning.

I'm going to bed in a minute, I said.

Me too, you said.

Neither of us moved.

The parcel was outside where we'd left it on the garden path. We were watching an I Love 1980s programme, one we'd watched twice before. We were talking about how it had become possible that there never was a miners' strike, a war, a right-wing landslide, a massive recession or any huge protest march; instead there were only Rubik's cubes, Transformers and a puppet TV compere shaped like a rat.

Snoods was 1983, you said. How old were you in 1983?

Seventeen, I said.

Tell me something that actually happened, you said. Something about you that I don't know, from when you were seventeen and I was sixteen and we lived in different towns and didn't know yet that each other had even been born.

I thought for a moment.

1983 is the year I was in love with Heyden, I said.

With who? you said.

Natasha Heyden, I said. But she only answered to Heyden.

You never told me about anyone called Natasha Heyden before, you said.

Heyden, I was saying. I haven't thought about her for years. She was in the year above me at school. There was this story about her and Mrs Brand the maths teacher, Mrs Brand was going round the class asking for answers and she got to Heyden and called her Natasha and Heyden acted like she didn't hear, so Mrs Brand asked her for the answer again and Heyden still acted like she didn't hear, looking Mrs Brand in the eye, and this went on for twenty minutes, the whole class watching, Mrs Brand standing over Heyden's desk hitting it with the flat of her hand saying the name Natasha Natasha Natasha and Heyden looking straight through her. Heyden wasn't like anybody else. She was terribly beautiful.

What did she look like? you said.

She was small and blonde and kind of wiry, I said. She shot things.

She what? you said.

She had some kind of rifle. She was a really good shot. Their house was out by itself on the edge of town, next to the fields by the ring road; there were a lot of rabbits, birds. I made friends with her little sister Angela Heyden so I could hang around their house on a Saturday, she had these sticking-out teeth. Angela hated Heyden shooting things, she used to hide in her bedroom with her stereo turned right up, Bonnie Tyler, Total Eclipse of the Heart on repeat, so she couldn't hear the shots. Every Saturday I would say I needed fresh air or a glass of water or something, and then I would slip out to their back garden knowing Angela would never dare come out and fetch me back.

So all the time I spent anywhere near Heyden was time that Heyden was killing things, or waiting to kill things, or finishing them off, laying out a row of dead things on their lawn. She acted like I wasn't there. It made me act like I wasn't there too. I would sit on the back step of their house. She'd be at the end of their garden, she'd lean over the fence then lift the rifle to her head, to her blue eye, and swing the length of it after whatever was flying or running. Most Saturdays I went to their house. Most Saturdays this same thing. Until one Saturday I got there and Angela Heyden answered the front door and took me upstairs.

Usually Angela Heyden and I at least feigned friendship when I got to their house; usually we had a cup of coffee or looked at her books or magazines, talked about school or homework or boys or whatever. She had these cards she'd made herself, she said they were future cards. They were just bits of paper, bits of card, they had words written on them and every week she would shuffle them, give them to me to shuffle for myself, then tell me to choose three and turn them over and these would be my words for the future.

What kind of words? you said.

I don't know, I said. I don't remember now.

You must remember one, you said. Tell me some.

Well I do remember I had the word luxurious

once, I said. That was good. I thought it meant I'd be very rich later when I was an adult and was married and had children and a job and was living in the kind of spotless fitted-kitchen house an adult is supposed to live in, doing a jet-set job, wearing suits, having dinner parties for articulate friends and striding across a beige beach with my family and my Dalmatian.

Uncannily like our life, you said.

I had the word astute once, I said, I remember looking it up in the dictionary and being pleased about it. I once got the word fiery. That was good. I was in a mood with my parents all that weekend about nothing, just to prove to myself how fiery I was.

Usually we would do this, or something like this, before I sloped off desperate to watch her beautiful sister killing things. But this particular day, nothing like that. Not a word. Not even a hello. Angela Heyden led me up the stairs. When we got up there she knocked on a door that wasn't her bedroom door, pushed open the door, pushed me inside and shut the door after me.

Was it Heyden's room? you said.

Heyden's room, Heyden's things, Heyden's bed, and there was Heyden herself at the window, her back to me and her gun against the wall. Be quiet, she said without turning round. Then she looked round and said, Oh, it's you. It was the first time she had ever. And then she made me kill the squirrel.

You sat up.

She did what? you said.

She waved me over to the window. It looked down on to their back garden. She pointed to the lawn and told me, hushed, that the cardboard box down there was balanced on a stick and then she showed me a piece of string in her hand, I could see it tightening in the air all the way across the garden. It was attached to the stick.

There's a mound of food under that box, she said in my ear. I've been training squirrels all week for you.

The thought that she'd been doing something, anything, for me made my heart fly up through my body, up it went into the sky and flew up and down like a summer bird.

If Heyden had seen it do that, she'd have shot it, you said.

So she moves along and makes room for me at the window, I said. And, sure enough, this grey squirrel with its brown paws and brown face comes stopping and starting over the lawn and goes straight in, like it's meant to, under the box and sits down there eating something. Heyden gives the string a tug and the box comes down over it.

Then Heyden hands me the rifle. And I do it. I did it. I shot at the box. I missed. I shot at it again. I shot at it four times. I hit something the fourth time. The box fell in on itself. I think I killed it.

You think you did? you said.

Natasha Heyden grabbing at the gun to reload it, yelling at me for missing then jumping up and down in her room when I hit the box, haring off down the stairs to see if it was dead or alive and me standing at the window, everything in my body shaking and my ears full of the noise I'd just made and Angela's Total Eclipse of the Heart playing down the corridor. I went down the stairs too. I went out their front door and up the path and away. I stood for a minute at the end of their road. I was shaking. I was mortified. But I wasn't mortified about whether I'd killed a squirrel or not; I was mortified that it hadn't even been able to run away and I'd still missed it, not once or twice but three times.

One way was towards home and the other was towards the flyover. I couldn't go home. When I got to the motorway I walked on the hard shoulder. I must have been halfway to the city. It started to really rain. I got picked up by a kind person. A woman stopped and said did I need a lift. Her car was quite new, it smelt new, she draped plastic bags on its back seat for me to sit on so I wouldn't mark the leatherette. She said I looked terrible and what had happened to me. I couldn't tell her about the actual squirrel or anything, it would have sounded mad. I'm dead, I said. My heart is gone. She laughed. She said I didn't look in the least dead and wherever it had gone it wouldn't be gone for long. She made me go home, she u-turned on the motorway to run me there. I can clearly remember the scraping noise the bottom of her car made on the central reservation when she did.

Then what happened? you said.

Nothing, I said. I never went back to Heyden's house. I heard about her afterwards; apparently she went off to college in Texas or somewhere.

She came back and got some kind of job in career management or maybe party politics, you said. She's probably in our government now. What happened to the squirrel? Was it dead?

That's the thing, I said. I never found out. I don't know.

What about the sister? you said.

I shrugged.

But you were lucky, you said. She was astute, that woman who picked you up in her car.

Yes, I said.

And fiery, that girl with the gun, you said. All that weekend killing. All because you could. How indulgent. How luxurious. How 1980s.

Ah, I see, I said. I get it. The future word thing.

Though actually, you said, it was her all along, the sister, Angela, not the other one, who was fiery if anyone was.

Angela Heyden? No way, I said.

Playing that heartfelt record over and over, so loud, you said. And it's Angela who was astute in the end. Knowing, finally, the nothing she was to you. Handing you over to her sister like that, so neatly packaged.

Ha ha, I said. But what about luxurious? You missed out luxurious. Was Angela luxurious too?

Yes, you said. She was.

Uh huh? I said.

Well, you said stalling for time. Well, she was, uh, luxurious with you. She gave you a great deal of luxury.

How? I said.

She was clearly in love with you herself, you said. And she gave you all those futures, all those possibilities of what to be. Three whole new future selves every week, she gave you. Until she finally gave up on you. What happened to Angela? I like the sound of her. Much more than her psychopath sister. I wonder where she lives now. I wonder if she'd do me some words. I wouldn't kill a squirrel for her, but I'd walk along a wet motorway for a girl like that any day.

I punched you in the side, quite hard. You laughed and wrestled me down on the couch and held me so I couldn't move my arms.

Ouch, I said.

Oh God, you said, backing off. I'm so sorry. Did I hurt you? Is your knee okay?

I had forgotten I was even supposed to be sore. Then it crossed your face and I remembered it myself, the original reason we'd forgotten or remembered anything tonight. The parcel of old bad-smelling cloth was outside our house in the dark.

We both sat up. I took your hand. You looked me in the eye.

What'll we do with it? you said.

We put it back in the post the next day. Two days later a postman returned it to our address.

We took it to the main post office and told them it wasn't for us. A woman accepted it through the hatch. She redirected it to the room where the questionable deliveries wait to be processed. After this it was despatched to the centralized depot, a building the size of several aircraft hangars on the outskirts of the city, full of undeliverables.

We took it to the police station. We told the man at the reception desk that it had been open when it arrived and that we had been disturbed by what was in it. The man put the parcel on one side and took down four forms' worth of details. He told us that people come into the station with dubious packets very often. He wouldn't tell us exactly what happened to parcels like the one we handed in. He said they were dealt with as fully as possible.

We put it in the outside bin. The following Thursday the binmen emptied it into one of the municipal trucks, which churned up the contents of hundreds of bins and delivered them to the landfill on the outskirts, where the parcel still is, under the acceptable statistically monitored municipal layers of waste.

We burned it in the garden incinerator. We stoked up a high-shooting fire with old dried offcuts from the bushes and the trees, then when the fire was at its fastest we threw it in and clamped the lid on. Its particles flew into the air through the chimney, over our heads, over the roofs of the neighbourhood.

We buried it in the garden. Then you remembered a poem where a man buries his anger and his anger grows into a poisonous tree and kills the person he is angry with. For days we worried about what might grow from it. We kept going outside to check. When the weather changed and we went into the garden less, we worried that in years to come, after we were gone, someone might be digging and might find it and open it like we had. Down below the ground it decomposed. Underground creatures ate at it and nested in it. Grass grew over the place we buried it and eventually we couldn't tell exactly where.

We went out to the garden at three in the morning and picked it up off the path. We brought it back into the kitchen. You sliced it open again with the knife. We held our breath so we wouldn't smell it. I emptied it all, including the note, into the washing machine and shut the door. We put the soap in the drawer and turned the temperature to 90°C. We stayed up while the machine churned through the cycle; it was light outside when we packed them, dried, folded, lightly paper-specked, back into their parcel and sealed up the knife-slice again. You wrote across it with an indelible marker NOT KNOWN AT THIS ADDRESS RETURN TO SENDER. We slept for three hours then got up and had breakfast, then we took it, me limping and sore, you bleary and exhausted, to our local post office, the one they are always threatening with closure because of cuts, and dropped it in the post-sack.

the first person

This, though, is a new you and a new me. In this particular story we are new to each other in the oldest way, well, it's certainly making me feel a bit on the ancient side. I'm not completely sure the body can take such bright new newness when, like mine, it's gone well past all the acceptable newnesses, the well-signposted ones, the ones we're supposed to have: the shiny teens, the know-all twenties, the greenhorn mid-thirties, the sudden shattering astonishments of forty, etc. But this. This is unexpected. Today I woke up and you weren't there. I came down and found the room strangely empty. Then I saw that the dining-room table had been dragged outside on to the grass in the sun, and you were sitting at it waiting for me with breakfast ready all round you.

I don't know that I'm up to this any more, I say.

Yawn, you say.

(You don't actually yawn, you say the word yawn. Then you look at me across the table and smile. I'm still unused to your smile, and to it being directed at me. Sometimes when you smile at me I have an urge to look over my shoulder to see who it is you're smiling at.)

I mean it, I say as I sit down, I'm not sure that there's much room left in my life for all this. I'm not sure there's enough patience in me. I'm a bit too, eh, old for it. I'm a bit too old, say, to be meeting anybody's parents. I'm the age of a parent myself, for God's sake.

Who said anything about parents? All I did was move the table and make some coffee, you say.

I'm definitely too old to have to do all that meeting somebody new's lifetime haul of dearest friends and so on, I say.

Okay, you say. Whatever.

Like going on holiday and finding yourself in a house full of shrieking strangers, I say.

Well, thanks, you say.

You know what I mean, I say.

Okay, so you're in luck, you say. I don't have any parents. None at all. I was born without parents.

Perfect, I say.

And I've hundreds of friends but they're all the kind of people who'll simply accept your presence in my life without having to have any back story. Lucky, eh? Liberating, eh?

Too good to be true, I say.

It'll be just as scary for me, meeting your friends, you say. Like, imagine. Imagine going into a really huge, high-windowed, wood-panelled, book-lined library full of really ancient books, thousands and thousands of them. It smells really nice, and everything, of all the old books and all their old pages –

You used the word ancient once and the word old twice there, I say. You're not perfect after all.

It's beautiful and everything, you say. But it's a bit like, I get in there and I look up and I know I've not read any of these books. And at any moment I might find I have to sit a really tough examination on all the things all the books in the whole place are about.

Crabbed age and youth, I say.

You look at me. You raise an eyebrow.

It's a quote, I say. From what we librarians call the library.

It's only ten years, you say. It's not that much. Well, fifteen. Ah, I get it. Is this like when we woke up and you turned and looked at me and said I was like a, what was it, the ice-hockey thing?

Puck, I say. I said it was like having Puck in my bed.

Yeah, a puck, you say.

Exactly the same, I say. Same library shelf ballpark. Ice hockey. Puck. Who'd dare mention Ariel after that?

Only mention Persil Non-Bio or I'll come straight out in a rash, you say, I'm very skin-sensitive.

You say it like a double bluff joke, so laughingly that I find myself wondering again if maybe you're having me on, you've been having me on all along, that really you know exactly who and what and so on, really you know a lot more than I do, about everything, but for some reason you're pretending you don't, though I can't imagine what such a reason would be. You're the perfect picture of innocence. You lean back in the chair, the chair up on two legs.

You'll fall, I say.

No way, you say.

You're looking at the sky. I follow your gaze and see you're watching the flight of the summer swifts; they're just back from the south.

Is it them that are the birds that sleep on the wing? you say.

Yes, I say.

Wow, you say. And never land on the ground? And keep flying and flying, and have to have their nests up high so they won't touch the ground, and have to keep the momentum going?

Yes, I say.

Imagine, you say. Like a song that never ended, like a constant ever-evolving music, like you'd just keep going and keep going with it, even when you're asleep.

You stand up; you stretch your arms in the air; you arch like a bow ready for an arrow.

Nothing in common, you and me, I say.

Yep. Nothing, you say.

We should just call it a day right now, I say.

Okay, you say.

You stand behind my chair and put your arms round me, then put them in under my shirt, your hands directly on me. You hold me very tight in under my clothes, and if there's a library anywhere near then someone just removed its roof, the shelves just flooded with sun and all the old books just remembered what it means to be bound in skin and to have a spine.

It's hopeless, I say.

Totally, you say behind me.

I can feel the silent laugh of you all the way up and down my back.

You're not the first person who ever made me feel like this, you know, I say.

I'm the first person today, though, you say.

You have peeled the roof off me and turned the whole library into a wood. Every book is a tree. Above the tops of the trees there's nothing but birds.

How am I supposed to survive this, out here in the wild wood?

The first time I saw you, you were eating an apple, I say. Well, almost the first time.

I remember, you say.

It was a Discovery, I say. You were just eating an apple as if there was nothing else to do in life.

There isn't, you say.

It is a little later the same day. We are back in bed. We have decided to invent a how-we-met story so that when we do meet each other's friends, round whatever table in whatever pub or restaurant or suburban dining room, we'll be protected. But the bit about the apple, and me seeing you, for almost the first time, eating the apple, is true.

It was in Departures, you say.

How do you mean? I say.

At the airport, you say. Where you were working at the time. You were wearing a lovely uniform.

Do they wear uniforms at Departures? I say.

They do, you say. I mean, you do. A quite nice uniform. I liked it, anyway.

And you were going round the world, I say. Were you going round the world by yourself?

I was doing a day trip round the world, you say. I wanted to see whether it was possible to do it in a day. And you were one of the security people working the X-ray machine where people's hand-luggage and jackets are checked for terrorism. And you asked me to take my jacket off.

And I saw, when you did, that instead of an arm, you had, like, a, a violin, and where your hand should be was the scrolly piece of wood at the end of a violin –

And I saw you staring, you say, and I looked at my arm and my hand and said, damn, here we go again.

And then I asked you to accompany me to the interview room, I say.

And I said there's really no need, it's just that I'm going through some changes, you say. Change is necessary.

Mutatis mutandis, I say. Mutability. Muton.

Dressed as lamb, you say.

Getting at my age again, I say. In my day, things were different.

Good. Change is good, you say. And then,

obviously, I had to take my shoes off for the shoe-checking machine, the special one that X-rays shoes –

And instead of feet, you had – I say.

Hooves, you say. Neat little ones, like the feet of a pony, or a donkey, or a goat, or a, what are they called? Deer.

Don't call me that, I say, it makes me feel old. And then I escorted you to the interview room and asked you would you assist me in filling out a form.

Very romantic indeed, you say. Our first meeting was very romantic.

Name, I say. Address. Age. Nationality. Occupation.

Occupation: hoofer, you say. I've hoofed it all over the world, me. It's a good life. It's what keeps me so young-looking. Right. That's what we're telling your friends, then. What about mine? What are we going to tell them?

They'll want to know about my long and interesting life before I met you, I say.

You put your head on my chest. You settle in my arms.

Go on, you say.

I was in the first flush of a new love, I say. I was having that surge of pure happiness and energy that happens when you're first in love again. I was whistling the tune of it, walking down a country road whose verges were all grasses and wildflowers, when I found myself alongside an old, old woman with a load of heavy-looking sticks on her back. It was picturesque. It was as if I were in another country.

The kind of country where there's no central heating, you say.

Yes, I say. And I said to her, can I give you a hand? And she stopped and said, are you absolutely sure you want to? And I said yes. And then I looked down at where my left hand had been and saw there was nothing there. I looked up my sleeve. I rolled the sleeve up. My arm ended in a stump at my wrist. I've changed my mind, I said to the old woman. I wonder if you'd mind returning my hand to me.

It was too late, you say.

Way, way back, the old woman was saying as she walked away out of the story, way back in my own day, I was just like you are now, you know.

Come back! I yelled. Give me back my hand right now!

Her voice came back at me over the top of the load of sticks she was carrying.

It's terrible, she said. What will you hold your fork with when you sit down to eat in polite company? How will anyone be able to tell that you're married? How will you ever play the guitar now, or ever again make a clip-clop sound like the hooves of a horse with two halves of a coconut? It's a tragedy.

The total fucker, you say.

You total fucker! I called after her. No I'm not, she called back. I've done you a favour. Now when you look in the mirror, you'll see a whole new person. You should be thanking me, you ungrateful little idiot.

What did you do? you say.

I stood and watched her go. I saw the bloody end of my sleeve at the end of my arm and I felt too faint to do anything. So I sat down on a large stone there at the side of the road. I sat in the summer birdsong and the strong scent of sun on cow parsley and I knew I'd have to get myself to a hospital soon. I mean, I'd like to be able to say that I sat there looking at the place where my hand had been and in the absence of just one hand I suddenly understood how imaginary characters might long for bones, I suddenly knew how dead people, if they can feel anything at all, long to be anything other than dead. But all I felt was outrage. All I felt was loss.

You kiss my breastbone. You reach and take my left hand.

Careful there, I say.

You settle your head on my chest again. You give my hand a little shake.

Your severed hand, however, you say, went on to have a happy and very fulfilled life. Like in all the best B-movies, your hand carried the personal characteristics of its owner with it. It could play sonatas by itself. It could not only ride horses but groom them efficaciously afterwards. It was good at playing poker, nifty at texting and googling, always deep in the pages of a good book. It was always putting itself in a pocket and bringing out change when anyone asked it for money in the street. It was also a renowned gigolo; it wasn't unusual for your hand to cross town by itself in the middle of the night, leaving one lover sated and happy in that after-love torpor, to please another, who was sitting up right then eagerly waiting to hold your hand. Also, you yourself became famous as a really versatile drummer. You were known the whole world over as Stumpy the Miracle Drummer. That's how we met. One night by chance I was contracted to play my arms off and hoof it in the very same bar in which you happened to be headlining. That afternoon, at four o'clock, rehearsal time, I came through the door of the bar –

You were eating an apple, I say.

It was a Discovery, apparently, you say.

I know, I say.

And we saw each other, you say.

So that's how we met, I say.

Yep, you say. Or how about this? How about we're story-free? How about, there *is* no story as to how we met?

(You walked past my door. I was sitting in the doorway reading my emails. I was in a bad mood because the night before I had stayed up late and found myself watching a repeat of a 1970s episode of Tales of the Unexpected; it was one I had seen thirty years ago in my adolescence and which I'd never forgotten. It was about a teenage girl whose parents have been killed in a car crash. She lives a rather unloved and abandoned life, and after a bad piano lesson with an unpleasant lady piano teacher, she is followed home to her unsympathetic grandmother's house by a sinister man. Someone is murdering adolescent girls. There are lots of shots of lakes being dredged and policemen with police dogs pulling against the leash in long grass. The next time the girl goes out, he's there again. He follows her again. To escape him she turns for help to a sweet old lady she meets by chance. The sweet old lady seems much more grandmotherly than the girl's grandmother. So the girl goes with this sweet old lady across a ragged wasteland to a caravan where the sweet old lady says she'll make her a nice cup of tea. The girl settles down. She feels safe for the first time. Then someone else comes in the caravan door. It's the sinister man. He's been in cahoots with the sweet old lady all along. That's where the story ends.

Thirty years ago, this thirty-minute story had terrified me. Thirty years on, the same story had made me very angry. It had sacrificed its girl character to a horrible end for the sake of a neat story; I had been arguing with the neatness and foulness and cynicism of it in my head all night. I had woken up still trying to think of alternative endings for the girl in the story, still granting her character a more open road, a kinder shape of things.

I was in the sun in the doorway, reading my emails. You walked past my door. You nodded hello. You had a case on your back, oblong, longer than your back. I heard you open a door up the road from my house. Then, not long after, I heard someone playing something beautiful on something.

It was a music I knew in my bones. It caught me out. It changed the air. It came into my house and made the room I was in a completely different place.

It was you.

I worked out which door you lived behind. I stood outside it. Something new was making me brave. I knew you were a bit younger than me. I knew I was a bit older than you. I knocked on your door. You answered. You were eating an apple.)

Ultimate liberation, I say now in my old bed with you in my arms. A story with no story. No adjectives. No beginning or middle or end. Ultimate freedom. Ultimate open sky.

No ultimates, you say.

Above our heads through the open dormer window in the slant of the roof of my bedroom: leaves, clouds, blueness, swifts.

Halfway through the afternoon I go into the back room and find you sitting in a square of sun in the window seat. You're reading a book. You see me and you lower the book.

Just trying to catch up a bit, you say. You wink.

I get it, I say. I've finally understood. I'm imagining you. I'm making this all up. You're not real.

Ah, you say. But what if it's me who's imagining you?

You're not the first person to spin me a yarn, I say.

I'm pre-yarn, me, you say. I'm post-yarn. Yarn.

You say the word yarn like you said the word yawn this morning. I try not to laugh.

It is early evening. We're in bed again. It is almost embarrassing, going to bed with someone so many times in the one day.

You're not the first person I've ever gone to bed with so many times in the one day, I say.

I hope not, you say.

You're not the first person I've ever felt new with, I say.

Won't be the last, you say.

You're not the first person to think he or she could save me, I say.

I'd never be so presumptuous, me, you say.

You're not the first person to squeeze whatever love juice it is you've squeezed into my eyes to make me see things so differently, I say.

Eh? you say.

Then you make the innocent face you make when you're pretending to be green.

You're not the first person I ever had really good talks like this with, I say.

I know, you say. Been there, done that. You feel very practised.

Thank you, I say. And you won't be the first person to leave me for someone else or something else.

Well but we've a good while before that, with any luck, you say.

And you're not the first person to, to, uh, to –, I say.

To stump you? you say. Well. You're not the first person who was ever wounded by love. You're not the first person who ever knocked on my door. You're not the first person I ever chanced my arm with. You're not the first person I ever tried to impress with my brilliant performance of not really being impressed with anything. You're not the first person to make me laugh. You're not the first person I ever made laugh. You're not the first person full stop. But you're the one right now. I'm the one right now. We're the one right now. That's enough, yes?

You're not the first person to make a speech like that at me, I say.

Then we're both laughing hard again in each other's new arms.

The day slips away without us noticing. It's summer dark outside. It's not long, by the looks of it, till the light will come up again.

On my way downstairs to make us some tea I see the dining-room table still out there in the garden on the lawn in the moonlight.

It looks unexpected. It looks unsafe, anomalous. It changes the garden. The garden changes it.

It strikes me, as I look at it, that the table is way beyond my control. Up until this moment, I mean, I believed I owned that table. Now, looking at it out in the open air, I know that I don't. I know for the first time that I maybe don't own anything.

If it rains tonight, the wood won't warp immediately. But if we leave it out there for long enough in the open air, it'll split. It'll buckle open. It'll stain. It'll have little tracks all over it where wasps and other creatures have gnawed at it for nest material. Its legs will sink into the grass, grass will come up and round the sides of its legs. Bindweed will find it. Heat and cold will ruin it. Greenness will swallow it up, will die down and spring back up round it, will make it old, ruined, weathered.

I don't know what I'll think tomorrow or the next day, but this is what I think right now.

It's the best thing that could happen to anything I ever imagined was mine.

Printed in the United States
by Baker & Taylor Publisher Services